BAD
COMPANY

By the same author

Run, Zan, Run

Missing

Dark Waters

Fighting Back

Another Me

Underworld

Roxy's Baby

CATHERINE MACPHAIL

BAD COMPANY

To

Fraserburgh Academy;

Catherine MacPhail

2006

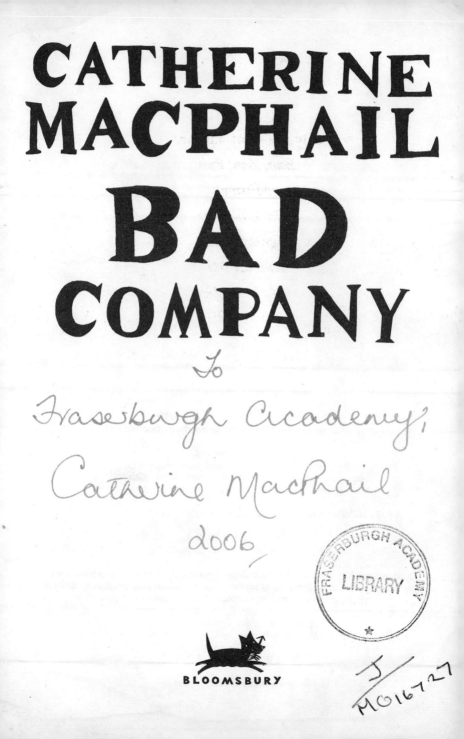

BLOOMSBURY

First published in Great Britain in 2001 by Bloomsbury Publishing Plc
38 Soho Square, London, W1D 3HB

This edition published in 2005

A CIP catalogue record of this book is available from the British Library

ISBN 0 7475 7830 3
9780747578307

All papers used by Bloomsbury Publishing are natural, recyclable products made
from wood grown in well-managed forests. The manufacturing processes conform
to the environmental regulations of the country of origin.

Typeset by Dorchester Typesetting Group Ltd
Printed in Great Britain by Clays Ltd, St Ives Plc

1 3 5 7 9 10 8 6 4 2

www.macphailbooks.com

For David and Suzanne

CHAPTER ONE

June 1st

What have I done? What have I done?

How did I ever get into all this trouble? I've never been so scared in all my life. Or felt so guilty. I've ruined Mr Murdoch's life, and he's never done anything to hurt me. He always liked me, though I can't imagine why. No one else does, and now, I don't blame them. Lissa Blythe, the wickedest girl in school. We've done a terrible thing, Diane Connell and I, and I don't know how to change it. I can't tell anyone the truth. No one would understand. We've been sent home. We'll probably never go back to school. Diane's right, she said they won't want us there now anyway. I feel like crawling into a hole and dying. I'll go down in history as evil and bad and . . .

I threw the diary across the room in my anger. Why was I writing in that stupid thing anyway? This is the worst moment in my life and I'm writing in a diary. Yet, my diary's the only place I can tell the truth. It's the only place I've ever told the truth since my dad went into prison. Was that when I changed? When I found out that my father, so successful, rich and going places, was really a crook and the only place he was going was jail? Or was it when Diane Connell came into my life? Diane Connell, my best friend. Or is she? Now, I'm not so sure. I'm so mixed up. I'm so unhappy.

I picked the diary up from the floor. It had fallen open at the entry for last December. How I remember that day. The day I found out that after almost three years my father was coming home from prison.

December 4th

I had just come in from school today when Jonny came screaming at me with the news. 'He's coming home, Lissa!' He was jumping up and down with delight. 'Daddy's coming home for Christmas.'

I ran into the kitchen to find Mum. 'Is it true? Is he coming back here? To this house?'

I refuse to call this place 'home'. This is the grotty little house we had to move to when he went into prison and our real house had to be sold, and the cars and the timeshare in the South of France. We lost everything because of HIM!

'He is your father,' Mum said patiently.

But I'll never call him that again, or Dad, or Daddy. His name's Jonathan Blythe, and I'll call him J.B. if I have to refer to him at all. I hate him.

'I don't want him here. Not for Christmas. Not any time.' I was yelling. I wanted to cry. But I wouldn't. Not for him.

'He's coming home and that's all about it.' Mum tried to smile at me, but she doesn't smile much any more and that's all because of him.

My mum's lovely, with her long, curly, dark hair and her blue, blue eyes. Irish eyes, J.B. used to say and he'd kiss her. He was always kissing her. Is that what she misses? Is that why she wants him back, so he can kiss her again?

She's lovely. Even though the smile has definitely gone from her eyes, she could get someone else to kiss her no problem.

'And Jonathan wants him back,' she went on.

'Jonny's daft.' And he is. Even though he's only eight I can tell he'll be daft for the rest of his life.

'And little Margo needs her daddy too.'

'Margo's not even three,' I shouted at her. 'He's been in prison since she was born. She doesn't even know him. So how can she need him?'

It was all so stupid. She was making excuses. It's Mum who really needs him. I want to hate her too. But I can't. She's my

9

mum, and while J.B.'s been away she's made our life good. I still get my dancing lessons, and Jonny goes off to cub camp every year. We go on holiday every summer too. Maybe not to the South of France like we used to. This summer it was a lodge in the Highlands. But it's all thanks to her. So why can't she see that we don't need him at all?

I tried to tell her that, but she wouldn't listen. All she said was, 'I need him, Lissa.'

The children of lovers are orphans, Mr Murdoch had once told us in English. I didn't understand what that meant until today, till that moment. They were still so much in love with each other, I didn't matter.

I was an orphan.

Reading my diary again, I can remember how angry I was. And even angrier when I went to school and discovered that it was all round the place that J.B. was getting out.

Nancy Ryman and Asra Bebbi were waiting for me at the school gates when I got there. I knew they were waiting for me though they were pretending not to. They used to be my best friends. Now I wouldn't even talk to them. When it had all come out about J.B. they had pretended they still wanted to be friends, still wanted me to come and sleep over at their homes. But I knew the truth. They were just feeling sorry for me. And I won't have anybody's pity. I promised myself that I would never set foot in their houses again. Nancy's dad is always in the local paper for his charity work. They say he's in line for an MBE. And Asra's father is a consultant at the local hospital. Oh, I'd really be out of place with them now. The only thing J.B.'s in line for is parole.

Nancy was smiling as I approached. 'Hi, Lissa. Asra and I were wondering,' she pulled Asra towards her for support. She wasn't smiling. I suppose she thought I'd snubbed her enough in the past. Nancy never gave up trying. 'Asra and I were wondering if you'd come to the Christmas disco with us. It'll be great fun.'

She knew about J.B. too. Both of them did. And they were feeling sorry for poor little Lissa. Well, no one was ever going to feel sorry for me.

'With you two?' I sneered. 'How could that possibly be fun?'

Nancy's face flushed. She swallowed. For a split second I regretted it. I wanted to go so much. Asra pulled Nancy on.

'Come on, Nancy. I told you it wouldn't do any good.'

I had a lump in my throat as I watched them go. In that second I would have shouted after them, but right then Ralph Aird yelled across the playground at me.

'I hear the Godfather's coming out on parole.' He couldn't ever leave it alone. I hated Ralph Aird, almost as much as he hated me. He was always chewing gum and trying to look cool. Scruffy was the word I'd use to describe him, with his baseball cap always turned back to front and his jeans that looked too big for him. He came from one of the worst areas of the town. His father had spent most of his adult life in one prison or another. Finally, ending up in the same one as J.B.

I ignored Ralph Aird. Dirt beneath my feet. I swept past him with my nose in the air. But Ralph didn't know how to keep his big mouth shut.

'I don't know how you can still be such a stuck-up wee snob, Lissa Blythe. Not when your daddy's slopping out in the same cell as mine.'

'He is not! He's got a cell to himself and a job in the library.' I had always insisted on that, even though I knew it was a lie. I was always telling lies about him.

'The governor knows he's innocent and he'll be out soon,' I used to tell everyone, believing that at least.

But of course, he wasn't. The papers screamed his guilt on the front pages, and he had confessed, quietly to Mum and me. I had believed in him. Made a right fool of myself sticking up for him, and he had let me down.

Ralph swaggered into step beside me. 'Know why I call him the Godfather?' He aimed that at his friends who followed along behind him. He always had a group of idiots, as scruffy as himself, who hung on his every word. I wanted to tell him to buzz off, but I knew he wouldn't. He never did. 'Because I remember our wee Lissa here telling me he was a big gangland boss. Head of the Underworld. The Godfather, see?'

I blushed to remember that I had. When I'd finally admitted to myself J.B. was guilty, I decided at least he could be a leader, in charge, top man. Well, I'd only been eleven then. I was bound to say something stupid. And anyway, at that point I was sure I'd be going on to Adler Academy, the private school on the outskirts of the town. I would never see Ralph Aird or his like again. So I could tell them anything. They'd never find out the truth. But Adler Academy cost money, Mum had told me, and money was something we just didn't have any more. So, after all my stupid lies, I was forced to go on to the same grotty High School as Ralph Aird. My stupid lies were found out and my torment got even worse.

Ralph was still rattling on. 'You even threatened to have me terminated, didn't you, Lissa?'

'Terminated? No. I would have had you put down,

Ralph. That's what you do to animals.'

Ralph ignored that. 'Some gangland boss. He ended up taking the blame for everything. My dad says that's called a "patsy". Too frightened to blow the whistle on his Big Boss. My dad says he's a laughing stock in that jail.'

That was it! I'd had enough of Ralph. I swung at him with my bag and caught him off balance. He staggered back and only saved himself from falling by landing on a couple of his friends.

'You've had it, Blythe.' He made a run at me, but I lifted my rucksack and swung it again at him. This time he did fall and, grabbing my rucksack, he pulled me down with him.

'Punch her, Ralphie!' someone shouted. So much for chivalry in this school.

'Shut that big mouth of hers.'

They were all against me. I didn't have a friend left in the whole school. Everyone had turned on me when it came out that my father was a crook. Not a master criminal. I could have lived with that. But the one who was caught. The stupid one who had refused to tell on anyone even though that would have meant a lighter sentence. Maybe none at all. No wonder they laughed at him in prison. No wonder I hated him.

I was ready to give Ralph another swipe with my bag,

but just at that moment we were both dragged to our feet by Mr Murdoch, Murdo, our English teacher.

'Ralph! Lissa!' Murdo has a strong Highland accent, with a lisp and a habit of spitting all over you when he talks, which is why nobody ever sits in the front two rows in his class.

His lisp was even worse when he was angry, which was often. He had a temper to match his fiery red hair.

'Lissa!' He lisped again, and I was showered with spit.

'It was his fault. It's always his fault.' I aimed my bag once again at Ralph. He sidestepped it neatly and winked. Of course, he wouldn't get the blame. Not Ralphie, not from Murdo. He thought Ralph had 'potential'.

Potential to be the next Hannibal Lecter is what I thought.

Murdo had thought I had potential once too. Once. Now, he always seemed to be angry at me.

'Get in there! I want to have a word with both of you!'

And with an angry push he sent us both flying towards the English classroom.

CHAPTER TWO

December 12th

I got detention today, thanks to that awful Ralph Aird. But I'll get him back one of these days, and then he'll be sorry. We were both dragged into Murdo's class and he bawled at the two of us at the top of his voice. I'm sure they could have heard him in Sydney, Australia. Of course, I got the worst of it. As usual.

'You will have to control that temper of yours, Lissa,' he yelled. He had the cheek to say that to me. He's always bawling at someone and whamming down his desk lid in his anger. 'You used to be a nice girl.'

At that point Ralphie sniggered and I almost walloped him again.

'People think you're a bit of a snob, I know,' Murdo went on, his voice a little softer now. He said it as if I had some sort of disease. If I'm a snob I have reason to be. I'm better than they are . . . or I used to think I was.

Murdo went on. 'But now . . .'

He hesitated and I filled in his silence. 'But now, I don't have any reason to be a snob, is that it? Now, I'm a jailbird's daughter. Just like him.'

'Actually, I'm a jailbird's son,' Ralph corrected as if he was being really smart.

'Neither you nor Ralph can blame yourself for what your fathers have done.'

'I don't,' I snapped back at him. *What makes him think I blame myself?*

'No one blames you.'

But they do. I can see it in their faces when they pass me in the corridors. And they're glad that it happened to me. To Lissa Blythe who always thought she was so much better than anyone else. I always used to be surrounded by friends, Nancy and Asra and me, we were always together. It took what happened to J.B. to make me realise how many of them only hung around with me because of who I was . . . or thought I was. A rich, successful man's daughter.

'I always hoped what happened to your father would make you a better person. More humble. It was all you were lacking, you know. A little humility.'

Humble? Me? Never!

'Instead,' his anger came back with force, 'it only made you worse.'

17

'You can say that again. See her, she's well spoiled, sir.' This came from Ralph, and he liked the expression so much he had to repeat it. 'Well spoiled.'

To my surprise Murdo told him to shut up.

'You're every bit as bad as she is!' he shouted at him.

He eventually let me go, but of course he kept Ralph behind to discuss the banner he is making for the district art competition. At the moment it stretches around the walls of the English classroom. A collage of *Great Moments in Literature*. He really needs Murdo's help with that one, considering Ralphie has never read a book in his life. Well, he has now, of course. He had to read them so he could draw the characters. The scenes go from some bloke getting his eyes poked out in *King Lear* (trust Ralphie to include that one. He's so bloodthirsty), to Harry Potter, pointing off into the distance to a future where books will always survive. (Murdo's words, not mine.) He's always painting new figures and attaching them to the banner. 'It's going to be a winner,' I heard Murdo shouting proudly. He was almost singing it with a happy Highland lilt. No wonder he was happy. It was Murdo who had first recognised Ralph's talent for art. 'His potential.'

I left them to it. But I had a miserable day. And it didn't help knowing that Ralph Aird, big-time loser, has more potential than me.

I was so miserable when I wrote that. I felt I had nothing in my life. And I was dreading Christmas, even if everyone else in the family was looking forward to it. J.B. would be coming home and my mum couldn't keep her excitement a secret. She was always cleaning the house so that everything sparkled. She had Jonny helping and even Margo tottered about with her little toy hoover. And how angry Mum was because I wouldn't help with anything.

But why should I have? I didn't ever want to see him again. Hadn't seen him for months. I stopped going to visit him in prison. It scared me. I was always so afraid they'd slam the door shut and not let me out just because I was *his* daughter. Mum didn't object to me not going. I know she hated taking us there. Not that Jonny minded. He thought it was an adventure. But as I've said before, Jonny's soft in the head.

He thought it was an adventure that Christmas too. Every time there was a knock on the door, or the phone rang he would yell, 'Is that Daddy now? Is he here yet?'

And he'd made a poster just to welcome him. He had it hung in the hallway of our poky little semi-detached and he had painted it with Mum's help, all different colours. WELCOME HOME DAD.

It made me puke every time I looked at it.

Even Margo toddled around, nose running, dragging her favourite blanket and sucking her thumb and giggling.

I spent most of my time in my room out of everyone's way. Determined not to get excited at the prospect of J.B. back in the house. Sitting in his favourite armchair. (Mum had always kept it.) Filling the bathroom with all his shaving gear. (He was always so untidy.) Or finding him and Mum holding each other whenever I walked into the kitchen, or the living room, or any room in the house. They were always holding each other. And I never wanted to see that again.

I wandered round the house after they left to go and pick him up. No amount of pleading would make me change my mind and go with them. This was to be my last few hours without J.B. here and I wanted to savour every second of them. We didn't need him here. Why couldn't he have stayed at one of those hostels especially for criminals who had just come out of jail? Why did he have to come here? Why did he have to be with us? Mum had bought the food in this house, with no help from him. She paid the rent. She even put up with the neighbours' whispered, sneering comments. He would only make things worse. He had no right to come back. As I sat in his armchair, and waited for their return, I grew angrier and angrier. I didn't want him back here at all.

And there right in front of me was Jonny's WELCOME HOME DAD poster. Taunting me, making a fool of me. Everyone else wanted him. The house wanted him. I was, as usual, the odd one out. Well, I'd show him. I'd show them all. I'd show just how unwelcome he really was.

I was lying on my bed when I heard the car pull up outside the house. I recognised the engine. It never sounded healthy. It was an old car, a cheap car. But all that Mum could afford. I heard Margo's giggling scream as she was lifted high in the air. Even Mum was laughing. I bet every neighbour was peeking out of their net curtains and having a good laugh too. A laugh at us.

Then I heard J.B.'s voice. The first time I'd heard it in such a long time.

'OK, Jonny boy, what's the surprise you've got for me?'

Footsteps hurrying up the path. Jonny's excited cries. 'Daddy, Daddy, Daddy.' The front door opened. 'Look what I made for you.'

I heard J.B.'s gasp and Jonny's excitement turned to tears. 'My poster, Daddy. My poster.'

'Who did that!' Mum screamed, but she knew already.

Her feet were pounding upstairs and she was shouting, 'Lissa!'

I lay on my bed and I didn't care. Didn't care that Jonny's hard work was all spoiled. Didn't care that his poster was hanging in shreds along the wall, where I had ripped it and torn it and destroyed it. I was glad.

I heard J.B.'s plea. 'Leave it, Liz.'

But Mum wouldn't. When she threw open the door her eyes were wild with anger. 'How could you, Lissa? You know how much that meant to Jonny. How hard he worked on it.'

I jumped off the bed to face her. I wasn't ashamed of what I'd done.

'I won't have a welcome banner anywhere in this house. Not for him. He's not welcome here – *ever*!'

CHAPTER THREE

December 25th

This has been the worst Christmas ever. Worse than when J.B. first went into prison and Mum spent the whole day crying, dragging us off to see him in that awful place. I can still remember the thud of the doors as they slammed shut behind us. I never would go back after that. No matter how Mum pleaded. And I tore up the letters he sent me without even reading them after that.

I thought that Christmas Day would be my worst ever, but I was wrong. This one was worse. It was worse having him here, with Mum laughing and sitting on his knee – how could she do that? And Jonny lying on the floor with him, playing with his big red fire engine. I saw a tear in Mum's eye as she watched a sleeping Margo draped across his lap in front of the television, while he too slept after Christmas dinner.

There was a tear in my eye too, but it was with anger.

'You haven't opened the present Dad got you,' Mum said later.

And I don't intend to, I told her. How could she think anything else? He's not buying me with a cheap present. 'I don't want anything from him. He's a crook.'

'You know he's paid for that, Lissa. He'll be paying for that for the rest of his life.'

Good! Why shouldn't he suffer, I thought, the way he's made us suffer.

He even tried to talk to me. He came into the living room while I was searching for a video to watch. He sat across from me, watching me silently.

I pulled out video after video, throwing them on the floor behind me, as nosily as I could.

'I don't blame you, Lissa, for not being able to forgive me.'

Ha! How kind of him, not blaming me. I don't think.

'I tried to explain so often, in the letters I sent you. Explain and apologise.'

Another couple of videos were thrown on to the floor.

He sat there still. Couldn't he see I wanted rid of him? 'I want to beg your forgiveness. I was greedy. The money was so easy and gave us all such a good life. I got in with the wrong people, though I didn't realise they were the wrong people at first. I thought it was the job of a lifetime, and when I was asked to cover things up, change a few items on the accounts, I kept telling *myself I wasn't hurting anyone. I suppose I pushed to the back of my mind that the kind of people I was working for didn't care who they hurt.'*

Was he just realising that? Because that had been the thing I couldn't take, couldn't understand. The people he was protecting, covering up for, were evil. They killed people. Contract killings, it had said in the papers, gangland bosses, mobsters. People you think only exist in old movies. And stupid old J.B. had gone to prison rather than tell everything he knew about them. I found the video I wanted right at the back of the cabinet. I pushed it into the recorder and switched it on, totally ignoring him. J.B. gave up then. He left the room without another word.

I wish I could run away. I wish I lived anywhere else but here.

If Christmas had been bad, going back to school after was even worse.

'I had the old man home for Christmas as well, Lissa,' Ralph shouted as I walked into the classroom. 'Did you have as good a laugh with yours as I did with mine?'

'Yes,' I said. 'But you had to press the suit with the arrows for your dad going back, didn't you?'

Ralph jumped from his seat and blocked my way. I only stared down at his big clumsy feet and said nothing.

'See if I was you, I'd keep that suit handy. He'll need it

when *he* goes back. They always go back. Look at my dad. He's spent more time in jail than he has with us. He's a serial jailbird. The leopard cannot change his spots. And your dad's another leopard.'

There was always that bit in me that rose to Ralph's bait. I never knew why. Why did I want to make J.B. look better than he was?

'Actually, J.B. is starting in another position soon.' I said it as if he was about to be made general manager of some big corporation. 'He's sifting through the offers right now.'

That only made Ralph giggle. 'Would that be the offers he can't refuse?' he said, referring to some old gangster movie.

But it was true. I'd heard my mother and him discussing it over Christmas. He had been offered a job. A position. 'I have to take it,' he had said. 'It's a start. And that's the most important thing. To earn money. To build my self-esteem again.'

His self-esteem. As if that was all that mattered.

I had just taken my seat when Murdo slammed into the classroom and almost threw his briefcase at the class.

He was in a bad mood. His face was red and his fiery ginger hair stood on end as if he hadn't combed it: either that or he'd had an electric shock this morning.

'There are people here who are not working hard enough.' His angry gaze surveyed the room, lingered for a second too long on me. 'The results of the tests you all did before Christmas were A-BOM-IN-ABLE,' he bawled. 'You will all do better this term or you will be suspended.' He paused, then his bawl became an earth-shattering roar. 'From the top balcony of the English corridor!'

To add more effect he slammed down his desk lid. The whole classroom shuddered.

Then, in that surprising way that Murdo had, he suddenly changed and beamed a smile. 'Let's hope our new girl will do better.'

The new girl had made the mistake of sitting right in front of Murdo, but as I watched her wipe her cheek discreetly with her finger, I knew she'd learned her first lesson and would never sit so close to Murdo again.

'This,' he hissed, 'is Diane Connell. Stand up, Diane.'

Diane did and turned to face the class. She looked a prim little miss, with what could only be called a rather superior smile. Her fair hair was held back in a china blue clasp and she had an expensive gold chain around her neck. I glanced across at Ralph. His lip was curled in annoyance as he watched her. He mouthed to his mates, 'She's a right wee madam.'

He didn't like her. Because of that, I decided at once that I did.

I didn't have any friends left in the school. Maybe it was time I made one. I smiled at the new girl, and she smiled back.

I didn't know then that Diane Connell was going to change my life.

CHAPTER FOUR

January 15th

I think Diane Connell and I are going to be great friends. She's so funny. She made me laugh five minutes after we started talking in the playground.

'Someone might have warned me about Murdo,' she said. 'I felt as if I was sitting under Niagara Falls.' And with that she plucked imaginary spit from her eye. 'He's disgusting, isn't he?'

Well, he is a bit, I had to agree. 'But he's nice really,' I told her.

She didn't seem to believe that. 'Nice? There's nothing nice about someone who keeps half his lunch stuck in his teeth. Was that broccoli? Or was it cabbage? Something green anyway.' She pretended to be sick on the playground.

She doesn't think our school is a very good one. She was in a much better school before, she says. And will be again, she told me. She's only here temporarily, till her parents find the 'right'

29

school for her. She made the little inverted commas with her fingers when she said that. The 'right' school.

'I mean, look at all these broken windows,' she said. 'And all that graffiti.' I tried to explain apologetically that the school had a lot of trouble from vandals. It's always being broken into and stuff stolen or smashed.

Diane had just said, 'What a dump.' Seeing it through her eyes, I realised with a shudder she was right.

Diane had to move here because of her father's job. He's just had a promotion. 'And what about your dad?' she asked me then. 'What does he do?'

I was so glad the bell rang just at that moment, and we had to hurry to our next class. I didn't want to answer that question. I didn't know what to say.

Because, maybe when she knows the truth about J.B., and she will find out – if I don't tell her someone else is bound to – she won't want to be my friend any more. And if I lose the chance of having a friend like Diane because of J.B. I'll never forgive him.

He was making dinner when I came home from school that day. At first I was determined not to eat it. But it smelt so good and I was *so* hungry that I relented – besides he makes one cracking lasagne. He always has. The very smell of it reminded me of days long ago, when he'd spend all his spare time in the kitchen insisting Mum relax and read her book, while he 'created a masterpiece'. I was the only one allowed in the kitchen with him. 'Only to you, my first-born, and heir to all I possess, will I pass on my secrets,' he would say. How he used to make me laugh. He'd pretend he was one of those TV chefs and I was his audience. He'd prance about and overact and . . .

I shook the memory away. It hurt too much. Because even then he'd been lying to us and cheating. A crook, and we didn't know it.

Margo sat in her high chair, her nose running, beating on her tray with her chubby little fists. Jonny was showing him the work he'd done in school that day.

'I had to write my diary. All about Christmas,' he said.

'Oh, that would be interesting, Jonny,' I said. I couldn't help sniggering. 'My Christmas list. I got a computer game and a fire engine . . . oh, and my daddy home from jail.'

There was a sudden, awkward silence.

'That's enough, Lissa!' Mum snapped. I was getting a bit fed up with Mum. It seemed to me she'd forgiven him too easily and she wasn't even trying to understand how I felt.

'I won't go back into prison. I promise,' J.B. said, spooning mouth-watering lasagne on to my plate. 'I'm fin-ished with all that.' It was an apology of sorts, but I didn't

et his eyes. 'I'm going to get a job soon. I've sent
letters and CVs everywhere. I've had an offer,' he
glanced at Mum when he said that. 'And I will take it if
nothing better comes along. You'll see, I'll get a good
job and I'll make you proud of me again.'

Mum touched his hand then as if he'd said something
wonderful. He bent towards her and kissed her. How could
she kiss him? And in front of her children. It was disgusting after what he'd done. If it hadn't been for me it could
have been like an episode from the Waltons.

Margo didn't seem to think it was disgusting. But then,
at two and a half she didn't know any better. I tutted loudly
to show them I didn't approve, but they ignored me.
Caught up in their own world as usual.

So, he was finished with all that was he? Lucky I didn't
believe him or I would have been disappointed. Next morning, after Mum had gone to work taking Jonny with her to
school, who appeared at our front door, but Magnus Pierce.

Magnus Pierce. He was the Big Boss that J.B. had
protected. Someone the papers described as 'a truly dangerous man'. The police, it seemed, knew all about him,
but could never get the proof they needed to put him
behind bars.

I will never forget the first time I met him. A big, imposing figure, he had come into J.B.'s office and sat on his desk as if he owned the whole place, (which, of course, I learned later that he did). He oozed richness and I liked that about him. Gold rings on both his pinkies, and a very expensive gold watch and diamond studs on his shirt cuffs. I could almost see my face in the shine of his brown leather shoes. I was fascinated by him.

'Hi, Magnus,' J.B. had greeted him like an old friend and they shook hands.

'Jonathan,' Magnus said and his clear, green eyes moved to me and smiled. 'And this is Lissa? Why, she's beautiful. She's so like your wife.'

(I'm not actually, I've got her hair and her eyes, but the ugly fizzog I've definitely inherited from J.B.)

If Magnus Pierce had tried to ruffle my hair then or pat my cheek I would have hated him, but he didn't. Instead, he held out his hand to me, just as he'd done to J.B. and introduced himself.

'I'm Magnus Pierce, Lissa. One of your dad's associates. Pleased to meet you.' He made me feel grown-up and special. How was I to know then just how vicious and horrible this man really was?

J.B. had shouldered all the blame for the fraud and dirty

dealings which were going on in their so-called 'business'. Just a front for all sorts of dodgy and criminal activities. He'd protected this man, Magnus Pierce. Instead of helping the police to put him behind bars where he belonged, he had protected him. And now here he was, back at our front door.

Had he watched for Mum going off to work before he arrived? I bet he had. He was certainly surprised to see me still there. When I opened the door to him he blinked. That was all, but it was enough for me to realise he hadn't expected to see me at all. Hadn't expected anyone to be at home but J.B. and Margo.

'You've grown since the last time I saw you,' he said.

'Yes. Growing up happens when you're my age.'

He smiled broadly, didn't seem the least offended by my cheek.

'Spirit. That's what you've got,' he said. 'And I like that.'

How had I ever been taken in by this horrible man? How had J.B.? He was sleazy. He had it written all over him.

J.B. appeared from the kitchen with Margo clutched in his arms. He didn't look too pleased to see him either. 'What are you doing here?' he asked.

'Jonathan,' Magnus Pierce stepped past me and into our house. 'So good to see you again.'

I wanted J.B. to turf him out. Tell him to go. I was disappointed that he didn't.

'Go to school, Lissa,' was all he said, dismissing me. I slammed the door shut in my anger.

It was all going to start again. I just knew it.

I was still feeling down about Magnus Pierce's visit when I got to school.

'Lissa? Is everything all right?' It was Diane, and she seemed genuinely concerned. It seemed she'd been waiting by the gates especially for me. 'You don't mind if I tag along with you? I don't know anybody else. And quite honestly . . .' she surveyed the playground with a sneer, '. . . I don't know if I like anybody else.' Her eyes rested on Ralph Aird who was heading a football against a wall. About all his head is good for if you ask me. 'Except for him,' Diane said. 'He's a bit dishy.'

I almost choked with shock. 'Ralph Aird? Are you kidding? Or is there something wrong with your eyesight?'

Diane drew her eyes back to mine. 'Oh, I know, he's so common. Not our kind of people at all.'

Our kind of people. I liked how she said that, including me in her special little circle. She didn't know about J.B., I thought. If only I could keep it that way.

We spent the whole day together, going from class to class, giggling and whispering. I put her in the picture about everyone. About Nancy and Asra and how they used to be my best friends.

'Why the "used to be"?' Diane asked. 'What happened?'

I had forgotten she might ask that. I coughed trying to think of an answer. Finally I just shrugged. 'You know what they say. Two's company. Three . . .'

'Always leads to someone being left out,' Diane finished for me. 'I don't like the look of them anyway.' And she steered me past them, her nose in the air.

I told her about the teachers too. Mrs Gregson, the geography teacher who was always locking herself in the cupboard. 'I'm sure she does it on purpose,' I told Diane. 'Just to get away from the class.'

'She's such a mouse, isn't she?' Diane said with a giggle. And she was, really, with her wisps of grey hair sticking out of a bun at the back of her head and her pursed, nervous little lips always twitching.

As she passed, Diane made little squeaking mousey sounds. I almost laughed out loud, but Mrs Gregson turned quickly and blushed. For a minute I thought she was going to say something, but she didn't.

'Of course, she didn't,' Diane said later. 'She's too much of a mouse.'

What really sent her into the giggles was the sight of Harry Ball, the fattest boy in the school, getting stuck in the turnstile in the school canteen.

At first I was a bit embarrassed, because Harry actually caught us laughing and he looked hurt.

'He deserves it,' Diane told me. 'He should go on a diet and lose some weight. Then no one would be able to laugh at him, would they?'

I had never seen it that way before, but now that Diane said it, it seemed so true.

Suddenly, a great voice boomed behind us. Murdo, and he had heard everything. 'With a robust personality like Harry's he needs those ample proportions.' He didn't look pleased. As Harry Ball tried to waddle past us, he grabbed him by the collar and dragged him round to face us. 'Yes, he is fat, isn't he?' He held him in front of us for our inspection. Diane didn't know Murdo, didn't understand his methods. She thought he was agreeing with us and she smirked. His voice suddenly roared. 'But one day,' he said, shaking Harry about like a rag doll, 'this fat boy will probably be running the country. He'll be Chancellor of the Exchequer with the mathematical brain he's got.' Harry's blush became a confident grin.

Murdo's angry gaze fixed on Diane. 'And what will you be doing then, Diane Connell? Hoping he won't be putting up your taxes probably. And wishing you'd been nicer to him at school so you could appeal to his better nature.' He grinned, with black spotted teeth. Black pudding had been on the menu for lunch.

'I won't have a better nature where they're concerned, sir,' Harry said, and shaking himself free he was off.

Murdo stared at both of us. The grin gone. I couldn't hold his gaze, but credit to Diane, she could.

'So, you've found a friend,' he said.

And I wasn't exactly sure which one of us he was referring to.

The day had gone well, until we were going home. Ralph and his cronies were waiting by the school gates. Diane linked her arm in mine and dragged me past them.

'Come on, Lissa,' she said. 'If we get any closer to this lot we'll need to be disinfected.'

Ralph sneered. 'You've found a mate, Lissa. Another wee snob just like you.'

Diane sucked in her cheeks and glared at them. She was good at doing that. 'Some people have every right to be snobs.'

'But not our Lissa,' Ralph said. 'Or hasn't she told you her secret yet?'

I wanted to run then. Get away as quickly as I could. But I couldn't move. I just knew what was coming next.

'You might not be so friendly with her if you knew what her daddy is.'

I wanted to run at Ralph Aird, punch him right in the gob.

Diane took her arm out of mine. 'What haven't you told me, Lissa?'

I swallowed. I wished the ground would open up and I could sink right into it. Ralph was smiling. Just waiting for the right second to give Diane the news.

'Lissa's dad's a jailbird, just like mine.'

CHAPTER FIVE

January 16th

Diane Connell is wonderful. My very best friend, forever. She totally proved it today, proved she's going to be the best friend anyone could ever have. When Ralph Aird told her about J.B., did she scowl? Did she walk away from me with her nose in the air?

Did she heck!

She looked at me. Looked at Ralphie boy and she lifted her eyebrows haughtily. 'Lissa can't be blamed for what her father is,' she said, smugly. 'Even if the likes of you can.'

He hadn't expected that. He thought she'd seemed so much of a snob he expected her to fling me from her dramatically and stride away with her pert little nose in the air. (To be quite honest, so did I.) Instead, she linked her arm in mine again, and with a giggle pulled me past Ralph and his moronic friends.

It will go down as one of the great moments of my life. I'll never forget Ralph's face as we ran off. Totally gobsmacked!

Later, she wanted to know all about J.B. and what he'd done. The gory details, she said. And I told her.

I've never really talked about it before, but I told Diane everything. How I felt about him being in prison and how I hated him now that he was out.

And Diane agreed with everything I said. We're so alike it's unbelievable. She'd feel exactly the same in my position, she said.

At last, I have a friend to confide in besides this diary.

The only thing I didn't tell her about was Magnus Pierce. He scares me too much.

'Can I ask you a favour, Lissa?' I remember now that J.B. came into my bedroom just as I'd finished writing my diary that day. I closed the book hurriedly and he glanced at it. 'You keep a diary now, do you?'

'Since I lost all my friends when you were sent to jail I had to have someone to confide in, didn't I?' That made him blush. And what favour could he possibly want from me?

He sat at the bottom of my bed. 'It's about Magnus Pierce.'

I felt my stomach churn. Even the mention of his name now frightened me.

'I don't want Mum to know he was here today. It would only upset her.'

'Yes, it would, wouldn't it,' I snapped back at him. 'Especially after all your promises.'

He was shaking his head. 'No. You're wrong, sweetheart. I didn't know he was coming. I told him never to come back here. I never want to see him, or hear from him again. You've got to believe that, Lissa. Just give me this one chance.'

Had he told Magnus Pierce all this? Or had Magnus Pierce come here to pay him off for keeping his mouth shut? That's what they did. I'd seen it in a movie once.

'If your Mum knows, she'll only worry. And there's nothing for her to worry about.'

I shrugged my shoulders. 'I don't care what you do.' And I walked out of the room and left him sitting there. I didn't say I'd tell Mum, and I didn't say I wouldn't. Let him stew for a while. Let him worry. It was about time he did.

But of course I didn't tell Mum. I couldn't bear the thought of her worrying. Even though it made me puke to see the way he hugged her in the kitchen and kissed her neck. He could always get round Mum no matter what he did. Well, it wouldn't work with me. He'd never get round me again.

Murdo was mad. Again. He had just had the results of our Christmas tests and they were dismal. We were a bunch of no good, lazy, useless, 'in-div-id-ualssss'. He spat out the words angrily.

Diane glanced at me and mouthed, 'So much for boosting our self-esteem.'

I giggled and Murdo's ranting halted abruptly. His eyes darted to me. 'Something amusing you, Miss Blythe?'

I swallowed and tried to think of something to say.

'Come here!' When Murdo was angry his accent became more Highland than usual. 'Come herrre!' he burred. When Murdo gave you an order, you obeyed. I stepped from the safety of my desk and sidled down the aisle toward him.

He always seemed bigger when he was angry, and broader. Right this minute he seemed to be filling the whole classroom.

I stopped in front of him.

'I'm glad you find all this so funny.' His glance went to Diane. He'd seen us stuck together like glue since she'd come to the school. At first I'd thought he was pleased about that. But now, his glare seemed to include her.

That put my back up. No one glares at my best friend.

'I'm not happy with your attitude, lass,' he said. I was

trying desperately to think of some clever retort, but all I could think of was that his breakfast was still embedded between his teeth. Bits of cornflake, and toast and a little sliver of grated cheese.

He shook his head with disappointment. 'Lissa!' he hissed, and he sprayed bits of cornflake all over me. 'What have you got to say for yourself?'

I wanted to say something clever, something so funny the whole class would laugh. I wanted to say something that would impress Diane. And it came to me in a flash of inspiration.

I pointed to the grated cheese. 'Are you keeping that for later . . . or do you intend to spit that all over me as well?'

I heard Diane giggle. But she was the only one. The rest of the class fell silent, except for an initial, communal gasp.

Murdo's face went even redder than usual. The anger seemed to leave him immediately. He closed his mouth and I realised in a moment that shamed me that he was embarrassed. Embarrassed and surprised.

'Stay behind after class,' was all he said, turning from me. 'You and I are going to have a little chat.'

No one in the class even glanced my way as I shambled back to my desk. They all kept their eyes downcast. Murdo was bad-tempered, and disgusting. But he was just about the most popular teacher in the school. Always striving to get the best out of us. Always pushing us to realise our potential.

Even Ralph, who sulked his way through most of his other classes came alive for Murdo.

Then I looked at Diane. Her eyes flickered across at me and they smiled. From under her desk she gave me the thumbs up, and I didn't feel bad any more. I knew I'd done the right thing.

As long as Diane understood.

CHAPTER SIX

January 30th

Murdo kept me back after class. He didn't shout. He didn't lose his temper. But a little nerve in his cheek kept throbbing all the time he lectured me in his low, steady, rhythmic Highland voice. And do you know, that was worse than any shouting.

'I've seen you snubbing people because you think you're better than they are, Lissa, which you're not. I've seen you patronising people because you think you're cleverer than they are . . . which you sometimes are.' He paused for a while after he said that. Studying me as if I was some biological experiment he didn't approve of. 'But I've never known you to be deliberately hurtful.'

I could feel my cheeks go red when he said that.

'What you said to me was cruel.' He waved that away. 'But I can take it. I have no prrroblems.' He rolled the 'r' around his tongue for an age. 'Prrrroblems.' 'Although you will never do it again,' he ordered me. 'But lately I've heard you being cruel to

other people. Harry Ball, for example. Laughing at him. You've never really done that before.' He hesitated again. He always does that when he wants to make you think about what he's saying. 'Before Diane Connell came into your life.'

That got my back up. All Diane's done for me so far is make me enjoy my life for a change.

I asked him if he was blaming Diane. He shook his head furiously and his hair went wild. I'm sure Murdo's hair has a life of its own.

'You know better than that!' he snapped at me. 'You don't blame anyone else for what you do wrong. Take responsibility for your own actions. I want you to think about that in future. Think before you do something just to please someone else.'

I might have done just that if, right at that moment, I hadn't heard a shuffling behind me. I looked round quickly and there was Ralph Aird. He was smirking and I wondered how much he'd heard. Too much probably.

He held out another of his cut-out figures from literature to add to the collage draped along the wall of the class.

Murdo immediately forgot me. He beamed a big smile at Ralph.

'Captain Ahab!' he yelled. 'That's brilliant, Ralph.'

Who on earth Captain Ahab is, is anybody's guess. But he comes with a whale. Ralph had made that too. Murdo was

47

delighted as he took it delicately from Ralph's hands and studied it. 'Your best ever. This is the prizewinner if ever I saw one.'

I didn't want to spoil his moment, but I'm sure Ralph got it wrong. Wasn't it Jonah who came with a whale?

Anyway, I was shooed away, totally forgotten and I left them attaching Captain Ahab and his whale to the collage, just like a couple of daft schoolboys.

Faithful Diane was waiting for me outside the classroom and she was furious.

'He's got no right to keep you back like that, you know. Not by yourself. Someone should be with you. A witness. Why he could say anything and who'd believe you if you complained? I mean, whoever's going to believe a pupil against a teacher?'

That is a very good point. She's really bright and smart, and best of all, she cares what happens to me.

When I look back, Diane made my life more than bearable over the next few weeks. I spent all my time with her during school and after school too. She invited me to her home, a big roomy house in the west end of the town. On a tree-lined street. It had a conservatory and a television room, a dining room and a morning room. Her father even had a wood-panelled study all to himself. I didn't meet him then. He was always off on business. But I met her mum.

She was very efficient-looking, a businesswoman too. She was stick thin and elegant and wore expensive silk scarves and lambswool sweaters.

I loved Diane's house, but it made me feel so homesick, reminding me so much of the lovely house we once had on a tree-lined street not too far from here.

'Your old man got a job yet, Blythe?' Ralph Aird shouted across the playground one day. He put on a posh voice. 'Or should I say a "position".' Then he laughed. It was more of a cackle actually.

Actually J.B. hadn't, and that was making me angrier every day. Mum was out working so hard and all he seemed to do was sit at home watching Margo and sending out CVs. But I wasn't going to admit that to the awful Ralph.

'He's got an "executive" position actually,' I lied. (Why did I always do that?) 'In a bank.'

Ralph Aird would never find out any different anyway, I thought. The only time he'd ever be in a bank would be to rob it.

He strode across the playground towards Diane and me. He looked smug. So smug I felt my stomach churn.

'Sure about that are you?' He said it as if he knew something I didn't.

'Of course I am,' I said defiantly.

He glanced around at his mates. They all sniggered. 'I think you should visit the supermarket after school. I think they might have a special offer on you'd be well interested in. Eh boys?'

He turned away and swaggered off, his mates trailing behind him, still sniggering.

'What do you mean by that!' I yelled after him, but he wouldn't answer.

I looked at Diane. 'What do you think he's up to?'

'Has J.B. started work in the supermarket without telling you?' She called him J.B. now too.

I shook my head. 'He's been for interviews, but he never gets anywhere. Who'd want to employ a jailbird?' I said. 'But he and Mum had been talking about some job he was considering. He'd said he might have to take it.'

'If he's only stacking shelves he might be too ashamed to tell you about it.'

He wouldn't tell me anyway, I thought. I never listened to him. Wasn't interested and I made sure he knew it.

'We'll both go to the supermarket after school. Check it out.'

That's the kind of friend she is, I thought.

'And if he is only stacking shelves, he'll get quite a shock when he sees you! He'll be the one who's embarrassed,' she giggled.

'I'll die if he's stacking shelves, Diane,' I said. After everything I'd always said about him. Stacking shelves!

'No you won't,' Diane said flatly. 'You'll just tell Ralph Aird he has got an executive position, but he's got to get shop floor practice first.'

'And anyway,' she went on as we filed in to our next class. 'you can't be responsible for all the humiliating things your dad does.'

That was funny. It was what Murdo always said, and I told her so.

She just shrugged. 'At least Rob Roy says some things that are sensible.'

But he wasn't stacking shelves. We walked all round the supermarket, looked behind the bacon counter and the delicatessen, at the checkouts and the bakery and he was nowhere to be seen. I began to think that maybe he'd been promoted already. Either that or Ralph Aird was having me on.

'I've had enough of this,' Diane said in disgust. 'Special offers. Two for the price of one. My mum would never shop here. She buys us all organic or free-range. Let's have a coke and just go.'

So we headed for the burger bar in the supermarket. Burgers A GoGo. Where everybody my age went for the music and to laugh at the teenage assistants with their funny hats with bulls' heads sticking out of them, and their stupid aprons. To make things even funnier they sped from table to table on roller skates. High Speed Service, it was called.

And that's where we found him. Looking ridiculous with a laughing bull sticking out of the top of his hat and serving Ralph Aird and all his cronies. J.B. the executive. I stopped dead and couldn't take my eyes off him. I would have run off then, but Ralph spotted me. He had obviously been looking out for me and he shouted loudly across the cafe and waved.

'Hey Lissa, honey, how's it going?'

J.B. was planting cokes on the table in front of them. I saw his back straighten before, slowly, he turned to face me. At least he had the decency to look mortified. Behind his back Ralph Aird laughed and mouthed to me, 'Executive position!' Then, to rub salt into it, he began to moo like a cow and all his friends joined in.

And then, as if all that wasn't embarrassing enough, J.B. began to roller skate toward me. I almost died. Didn't he know how stupid he looked? Didn't he care? I turned and ran out as fast as I could. Didn't turn even when he called after me.

I felt like crying. I was ashamed and angry. Ashamed of J.B. and angry at Ralph Aird.

And at that moment I don't know which of them I hated more.

CHAPTER SEVEN

March 8th

How can I ever face Ralph Aird again? Ralph Aird, the scumbag of the school with a father to prove it – or so I'd always thought. But am I any better than he is? Is this God getting his revenge on me for being so rotten to Ralph in the past? Well, I don't deserve it. Thank goodness for Diane. She ran with me outside the supermarket and stayed with me while I cried my eyes out. I've never cried in front of anyone before, but I can do it with Diane. She understands. 'I don't blame you for hating Ralph Aird,' she said. 'He's just so glad to see you in the same boat as he is now.'

And do you know, I'd never really thought about it like that. But it's true. That's why he's always got that smirk on his face. 'But you're better than he is, Lissa,' Diane told me. 'You can rise above him. He's a low life. Common as the muck on the bottom of my shoe.'

To make matters worse Ralph Aird couldn't let it be. He came out of the supermarket and stared taunting me. 'Your dad's coming out with the boys and me next week. We're going roller-blading. He's even going to give me a loan of his hat!' And he and his mates started circling Diane and I and laughing.

But Diane's a true friend. She pushed them out of the way with a sneer. She can look like a queen sometimes, a queen who is about to have someone beheaded. Someone like Ralph Aird. 'You're better than he is, Lissa. Better than all of them.'

That's what makes Diane so special. She always makes me feel so good, so proud of myself. That's a true friend.

'And as for your dad,' she snapped as we hurried away from Ralph's taunts.

J.B. I corrected her. I'm divorced from him now. If mums and dads can get divorced, then so can I.

'I know how I'd feel if my dad worked in a place like that. Wore a funny hat and looked so stupid.' She shivered at the very thought of it. 'I'd feel exactly the same way as you do. I'd hate him.'

She is so right. We're so alike. It's all J.B.'s fault, and Ralph Aird's. I hate them both.

J.B. tried to talk to me that same night. Mum suddenly had to go for a walk with Jonny and Margo, so we could be alone.

He switched the TV off and pocketed the remote control, obviously not taking any chances that I'd volume him out.

'I'm sorry about today,' he said at once, pacing nervously up and down the living room. 'I should have told you I was starting work there.'

'You call that working,' I jeered at him.

'Yes. I call it working,' he said. 'I'm being paid and I work really hard for my money.'

'Do you get extra for looking stupid?'

He tried to make a joke of it. 'I do look stupid, don't I?'

There was no answer to that. It would be useless even talking to him. I stood up to leave the room. 'It's not permanent, Lissa. I'll get something else, but for the moment, I'll work at anything. I almost had to beg them to give me a try there,' he tried at a laugh again.

He almost had to beg them? Was that supposed to make me feel better? It only made me feel more ashamed of him.

'I just want to earn money. To keep out of trouble.'

'It's always what you want, isn't it?' was all I said to him. 'You don't care how much you embarrass me.'

I pushed past him. He still tried to talk on, but I wouldn't listen.

'It won't be for long. I'm waiting for word about something else. A good job. Something better.'

His last words followed me as I bounded upstairs.

I slammed the door of my room so hard the house seemed to shudder. I wanted to cry, but I wouldn't. Not because of him. Instead I threw myself on the bed and started to think.

And do you know, what he said began to make sense. Working should be all that matters. If he had a job, any job, there would be less chance of Magnus Pierce drawing him back into his clutches.

A chance of another job? A better job? Was that the truth, or was he telling lies just like I always did? If it was the truth, maybe I'd been too hard. Maybe, I thought, I should go back downstairs and just sit with him. Nothing dramatic, like throwing my arms around him and begging his forgiveness. But maybe, just to sit with him would let him see I was ready to take one small step.

I was halfway down the stairs when I heard his urgent, whispered voice on the phone. 'Don't phone here any more. I can't take the risk. I'll get in touch with you.'

He replaced the receiver hurriedly and walked guiltily into the kitchen, closing the door softly behind him.

All my loathing for him returned. He was still in touch with them. Secret calls, like the ones I could remember from so long ago. Whispered calls.

'I'll get in touch with you.'

It wasn't finished. Magnus Pierce here in the house, and now this. He'd never change. Like Ralph Aird had said, the leopard never changes his spots.

The hardest thing I'd ever had to do was go to school next day. Even harder than the day so long ago when the whole story of J.B. broke in all the papers. At least then the teachers understood, especially Murdo. He had done his best to protect me from all the unwanted attention, asking me to stay in his class to help with a class project, giving me a lift home.

Today, there would be no one to protect me.

But I was wrong.

I still had Diane.

Ralph had spread the word to everyone and as I walked into the playground half the pupils who were hanging around the school gates immediately started mooing like cows.

Ralph sauntered up to me like a cowboy. 'How d'ye like your steak, honey?' Then he threw out his answer with a cowboy yell. 'Just yank off the horns and put it on a plate!'

Everyone burst out laughing at that. I'm sure I would have cried, wouldn't have been able to stop myself when suddenly, there was Diane pushing past Ralph with such force he stumbled and almost fell. He just glared at her.

'Hey Connell, watch it!'

She ignored him. She put her arm in mine and pulled me on. 'Come on, Lissa, let's get away from this low life scum.'

It was a wonderful moment. She gave me all the strength I needed to stare right back at Ralph Aird and his nerdy friends. I was better than them. Even if J.B. had shamed me I would always be better than Ralph Aird.

'You think you are something, Lissa Blythe,' he rasped at me.

I grinned back at him. 'You are something too, Ralph Aird, but I'm too much of a lady to tell you what it is.'

Then, with a cowboy yell of our own, Diane and I raced off.

'Thanks, Diane, that was brilliant,' I told her as we went into class. 'That'll show Ralph Aird.'

'No, it won't,' she said thoughtfully. 'Someone like him has to be taught a lesson. We've got to bring him down a peg or two.'

Always with Diane it was 'we'. Whatever hurt me, hurt her. She was definitely, I thought then, the best friend anyone could ever have.

'Yes, but what could we possibly do to Ralph Aird?'

She sucked in her cheeks, a sure sign she was thinking hard. Her brain was working. 'We'll think of something,' she said at last.

Murdo was in a great mood that morning. He beamed a big smile around the class, and it was all thanks to Ralph Aird. His banner was almost finished. And even I had to admit it looked impressive.

'By next week,' Murdo bellowed, 'it will be down off the wall, and in for the competition, and I think it has an excellent chance of winning. It's imaginative. It's clever, and it takes us on a journey through the world of books.' He aimed his smile at Ralph. 'You've done a wonderful job, Ralph. Come up here with me and bask in your class's admiration.'

Ralph shuffled out of his seat, his neck crimson with embarrassment, and possibly with pride too.

I thought he looked smug.

Murdo put a hand on his shoulder and pointed to the collage.

'Ralph read all these books you know. So he could really get to know the characters he was drawing.' This was Ralph Aird who had probably never read a book before in his life. Ralph looked even more embarrassed. 'And what wonderful characters he chose.' Murdo's voice rose with enthusiasm.

I looked at the collage too, at Oliver Twist asking for more and Captain Ahab and the great Moby Dick (Murdo had, by that time, told us all about him), at Long John Silver complete with parrot. And Harry Potter pointing off into the distance to a future where books will always be. The cut-out figures were alive and colourful and seemed as if they were ready to leap from the wall. Ralph had talent. Murdo had found it. So why did it make me so angry?

'If Ralph doesn't take the prize home for this school, I'll lay an egg.' Murdo laughed heartily. Only Diane and I didn't join in. 'So, now, I would like you to join me in congratulating Ralph for all his hard work and wishing him all the best in the competition.'

He began to clap. One by one the class joined him enthusiastically. Once Ralph had been really unpopular. Lots of people still thought he was obnoxious, but they also admired how hard he had worked. Ralph tried not to beam with delight. Everyone applauding Ralph Aird? My stomach tightened with something more than anger.

Reluctantly, Diane and I began to clap too, but our hearts weren't in it.

Yet Diane was smiling. I was puzzled by that smile, until we were filing out of the class and she pulled me close to her and whispered, 'Now, I know exactly how we can hurt Ralph Aird.'

CHAPTER EIGHT

March 9th

'There's no time like the present,' that's what Diane said. She says her dad always says you never put off till tomorrow what you can do today.

But I suddenly wanted to put it off forever when I heard what she had in mind. Destroy Ralph's collage! Rip it to shreds, tear it to pieces. It would all be blamed on the vandals who had been terrorising the school and the neighbourhood. That's what Diane said.

We sneaked back into the empty English classroom after the school had emptied and all we could hear were the cleaners rattling their mops and buckets in the corridors below.

I was breathing so fast I thought my heart was going to burst. I didn't want to be there. I'd tried to tell Diane but she wouldn't listen. But as I looked at the collage and realised the amount of work that had gone into it I wanted to be there even less.

Diane pushed a massive pair of scissors into my hands. 'I took them from the art class,' she answered to my surprised look. 'Now hurry, you haven't got much time.'

That was when I realised that Diane wasn't going to help me. I was meant to do this on my own.

'It's your revenge, silly,' she said. 'It'll get all that anger, that frustration, out of your system. My dad does it all the time. He's got his boss's photo on a punchball in the basement gym. And when that boss of his really gets his back up, he punches lumps out of his picture.' She laughed, covering her mouth so she wouldn't make a sound. 'Well, it's better than punching lumps out of him, isn't it?'

And wasn't this much better than punching lumps out of Ralph Aird?

'You wouldn't want to do Ralph any real harm, would you?' She seemed shocked at the thought of it and I hurried to correct her.

'Of course, I wouldn't.'

'Well, material things don't matter and this collage is only a material thing, isn't it?'

She was right, material things aren't important. I opened the scissors, but I still couldn't bring myself to make that first cut.

Diane was getting mad at me by this time. 'Goodness, Lissa. If you don't hurry up the cleaners will be on this floor.' She tutted in annoyance. She would never be this indecisive. Not Diane. I was letting her down.

'Oh well,' she said. 'Just don't come running to me moaning about Ralph Aird and how he made a fool of you, and how he humiliated you. It seems to me you'd let Ralph Aird walk all over you and you wouldn't do anything about it. Maybe you're more like your father than you like to think.'

But I wasn't like J.B. I wanted to shout that out to her.

'If Ralph Aird was in your shoes, I bet he wouldn't be holding back.'

And he wouldn't. Not Ralph Aird. He'd be destroying everything with whoops of delight. That, I suppose, decided me.

I snapped the scissors shut and cut Harry Potter in two.

As Diane hurried to the class door to keep watch, I heard her sigh with satisfaction. 'Thatta girl, Lissa.'

That first cut was the hardest. After that I snapped and slashed in a growing frenzy of anger. So much for Ralph Aird, and the way he'd made a fool of J.B. . . . Oliver Twist's head shot to the floor. So much for Murdo, and how he'd lost all faith in me . . . Moby Dick dangled from the banner like a broken concertina. So much for J.B. and all his lies . . . Fagin was sliced into ribbons. So much for everybody! Scheherazade and Huckleberry Finn were snipped and shredded like so much confetti.

So much for them all.

I was breathing hard by the time I'd finished and the

classroom floor was littered with the tattered remnants of Ralph's literary collage.

I could feel beads of sweat running down my back and I was shaking.

'Good work!' Diane said, patting me on the back and pulling me from the class. 'Now let's get out of here before someone sees us.'

I'm still shaking now. I can't stop.

What will I do if they ever find out it was me?

How could I ever have done such a terrible thing! Yet, I remember at the time thinking it was the best thing I could do. I can remember the rush of excitement I felt when I'd finished. Am I really such a nasty person?

I remember the fear too, the fear that someone would find out what I'd done. I didn't want to go to school next day. If it hadn't been for knowing that Diane would be there to support me, I don't think I would have gone.

She was waiting for me when I walked through the school gates next morning. She winked and whispered, 'It's all over the school. The cleaners found it this morning, and, know what? The vandals *are* getting the blame. Didn't I tell you?'

English was our first subject and as we filed in there

were gasps of horror from the rest of the class. Like coloured snow the shreds of the collage lay pathetically around the floor. They still hadn't been cleaned up. I couldn't see Ralph Aird at first. I didn't even look, so sure that guilt was written all over my face.

In the bright light of the morning what we had done seemed so much worse. The faces of the characters, lying askew all over the floor, jumped up at me accusingly. It seemed pathetic and sad. Murdo came striding into the room, slamming the door behind him. I have never seen him so angry. His wild hair stood on end as if he'd been pulling at it with his short stocky fingers.

His voice echoed round the class like the desperate wail of a banshee. 'How could anyone do such a cruel, senseless thing?'

He knew it had been me. At that moment I was sure of it. I couldn't meet his eyes and kept mine fastened on the desk in front of me. Trying hard not to listen to his words, finding that impossible.

'What kind of people do things like this? To destroy something beautiful is bad enough. But we know all the hard work, the care, the time that has gone into this beautiful work of art. We know how hard Ralph worked, all the enthusiasm he put into it.' Suddenly his voice became once more a terrifying bellow and he lifted his desk lid and slammed it down hard. 'And some pathetic idiot who has nothing in his life comes along and in the space of sixty seconds destroys something wonderful!'

Sixty seconds. That must have been how long it took. I had been frenzied, like someone crazy. And I hadn't once thought of it like that. All his care, all his enthusiasm. I had destroyed that too.

I felt my eyes pool with tears, but then half the class were crying. Diane turned to me. Was she crying too? She was sniffing and she said softly, 'I know, Lissa. How could anybody be so rotten?' And if I hadn't known the truth, I would have believed she meant that.

Murdo kept Ralph behind after class. It was my first chance to actually see Ralph's face. He had been slouched down in his seat, silent the whole lesson. Now, I saw for the first time that his face was chalk white. He stood in front of Murdo and Murdo's voice was soft and comforting. I hung back at the door and watched.

'There are no words for how I feel, Ralph. For what I could do to these people who did this.' He paused. Spittle was bubbling through his clenched teeth like lava ready to erupt from a volcano. 'This was a hellish act. But we can start again, Ralph. There's always next year's competition.'

I could only see the side of Ralph's face. 'It doesn't matter, sir,' he said in a flat, lifeless voice. 'My dad's right. He says there's no point even trying. Nothing ever works out for people like us.'

And though I could only see the side of Ralph's face, it was enough to make out a trickle of a tear.

That was when Murdo noticed me. His wild eyes fixed on mine. I felt my whole head go red, not just my face. He knows, I thought frantically. He must know. I ran out of the classroom, bursting through the doors that led out on to the playground.

'I don't know why you're so upset.' Diane sounded annoyed as we left school that day. 'It's done now. And he can always make another for next year.'

I thought about Ralph and what he had said. 'There's no point even trying.'

'Maybe he won't,' I said.

Diane shrugged. 'Well, if he doesn't that's his problem.'

'Maybe we should just confess and face up to it.' The thought terrified me.

'You must be joking!' For a moment a different Diane flashed in her eyes. One that kind of frightened me. Then she smiled. 'I mean, I would get into as much trouble as you and that wouldn't really be fair. I never really did anything. I was just the lookout.'

'I won't mention you. I promise.'

She was already shaking her head. 'That's not fair, Lissa. You don't do that to a friend. You do still want to be friends, don't you?'

And of course I did. Diane was the only friend I had. I couldn't bear the thought of losing her.

She was right anyway. It was done. Me confessing wouldn't help Ralph Aird. Diane said if he was made of good stuff he would bounce back. Make another for next year's competition. That's what Diane would do, she said. That's what people like us would do.

That's what I kept telling myself too.

If only I could forget his lifeless voice, with no hope left in it and that single tear running down Ralph Aird's face.

But all thought of Ralph Aird was blotted out when I came home. Magnus Pierce was there. Magnus Pierce with his big frame blocking the doorway into the living room. Margo was in her playpen, hugging a brand new teddybear. No prizes for guessing who had brought that. J.B. was standing over her, like a lion protecting his cub.

'We really have to talk,' Magnus Pierce was saying as I walked in. 'If I can't come here, you should come to my office. We have things to discuss.'

J.B. saw me then, and his eyes flickered in my direction. As they did Magnus Pierce turned slowly round.

'Ah, it's the lovely Lissa.' He beamed a big white smile at me. I almost expected to see his teeth flash like in a cartoon. 'And I'm just leaving. What a pity.' As he stepped past me he touched my shoulder and turned back to J.B. 'Just think about what I said, Jonathan. You'll see I'm right.' Then he paused and added very slowly, 'You have a family to look after you know.'

At that very moment Mum burst into the house with Jonny in tow. She'd known she was going to find Magnus Pierce here, must have seen his car. I certainly hadn't but then I had been too busy thinking about Ralph Aird.

'I'm just going, Mrs Blythe,' he said pleasantly, as if Mum had already asked him to do just that.

And in two long strides he was out of the house and moving down the path. Mum ran to J.B. and he held her close. Jonny looked baffled, didn't know what was going on. And Margo with her nose running was biting obliviously into her new bear.

Mum was crying. I could hear it in her voice though I couldn't see her face crushed against J.B.'s chest.

'I'm so afraid of that man, Jonny,' she said.

And do you know what J.B. said? 'So am I.'

CHAPTER NINE

April 3rd

I've been to Diane's house for dinner tonight. We went straight after school, running through streets and alleys and on to the broad tree-lined avenue where Diane lives. Our house had been in a street just like hers. Our house had been so much like hers. No wonder I love going there.

Dinner was served at a long, mahogany table and the dinner set was white china with dainty lines of gold around the edges. Tall crystal glasses were on the table for mineral water and stemmed glasses for the wine. In the middle was a bowl of glorious chrysanthemums. It took me back to the dinner parties Mum and Dad used to have for J.B.'s business partners. Magnus Pierce was always there. He seemed to dominate the table with his loud voice and his larger than life frame. Even then, he fascinated me.

And for the first time I have actually met Diane's dad. He has grey hair, but a young face and he looks so much like Diane, it's uncanny.

'Terrible thing about what happened to that boy's artwork,' he said while we were having dessert. (Banoffee pie, my favourite.) I almost choked on it. I glanced at Diane but she didn't even look up at me.

'They've locked the school up now, Daddy,' she said, sounding sorry for herself. 'It's like a prison in there. Isn't it, Lissa?'

My mouth was too dry to answer. Just as well I didn't have to. Diane's mum crashed into the conversation angrily. 'Locking up schools! Vandalism!' Her thin voice was shaking. 'I hate using clichés but I don't know what this world is coming to.'

Mr Connell was calmer. 'Yes, dear. But it won't be for long. We should hear from Adler Academy soon.'

Adler Academy, the private school in the countryside nearby. The one I had once hoped to attend.

Now Diane is going to Adler Academy. Leaving me alone again? I can't bear the thought of it. It was only just before I was leaving for home that I had the chance to ask her about it.

'Well, you didn't think I'd be staying in that dump, did you?'

And of course, I shouldn't have. Diane was never meant to be in a school like mine. But the thought of losing her just makes me feel sick.

'Couldn't J.B. send you to Adler Academy with me?'

74

Sure, I almost said. He'll be able to afford it with his tips from Burgers A GoGo. He has a night job now too, stacking shelves. It gets worse and worse.

But he has an interview coming up, for a 'good position'. I heard him discussing it with Mum. And if he gets that job, then why shouldn't I ask him to let me go to Adler Academy with Diane?

How sure I was when I wrote that. Sure I was safe. Sure Diane was my friend. Sure everything was going to be all right. Diane was the only thing that made school bearable. Security had been tightened up because of what had happened, and there was an air of mistrust about the place.

I was convinced Murdo knew I was responsible. He never smiled at me any more but I found he was watching me, very thoughtfully. When he talked to me he was always brusque.

I didn't care any more. I had Diane. And she had been right. No one had blamed us. Everybody assumed it had been the vandals and soon everything settled down once again.

Except for Ralph Aird. Diane said he had reverted to type.

He was always missing school and when he was there

he was sullen and bad-tempered. Even Murdo couldn't motivate him.

At moments like that I felt sick with guilt. Had I done that to him? How would he have acted if he'd won the competition? Proud? Confident? A totally different Ralph?

And he would have won. Murdo stormed into the class one day and showed us the entry that did win. A very unimaginative paper tower covered with 'My Favourite Words from Books'.

Murdo was incensed that such a winner had been chosen. It was banging down the desk time again. 'Words are nothing!' he shouted, his Highland burr always more noticeable when he was angry. 'It's how they are used that matters. The ideas they convey.' He spat the words out at us. 'It's the characters they create. Ah Ralph! Your entry spoke of characters and ideas and literature.' He shook his head violently and addressed Ralph's empty chair as if he was in it. 'Ah Ralph, surely you would have been the winner instead!'

Later that same afternoon as we passed two of the other teachers in the corridor we heard them discussing Ralph. Diane pulled me back to listen.

'He's not at school again. And I heard he's been running

wild at night time all through the town centre. Always said he was a bad lot.'

The other teacher agreed. 'Well, look at the family he comes from. You know, I wouldn't be surprised if he'd destroyed that collage himself. People like Ralph Aird and his kind can't handle that kind of responsibility. But don't tell old Murdo I said that, you know how precious he thinks his pupils are.'

They moved off still talking and I wanted to scream after them, 'He didn't destroy it. He didn't. We did.'

But Diane thought it was amusing. 'Told you they'd never suspect us,' she said.

'But that's so unfair, Diane. If they start to think he did it himself.'

But she just shrugged that off. 'Do you think Ralph Aird cares? He's probably forgotten his old collage already.'

I didn't think that was true somehow, and as I trudged home it was all I could think about.

I could hear Margo snoring as I let myself in. She was lying on her back in her playpen, sounding like a great navvy. 'She's got adenoids,' Mum keeps insisting. I stood looking at her for a moment. Apart from the awful noise, and her runny nose, she looked so sweet with her chubby cheeks and her rosebud mouth. I warmed all over just watching her.

But where was J.B.? Not far anyway. He'd never leave Margo alone. Yet the house seemed so quiet. Ominously quiet.

He wasn't in the kitchen. The lunch dishes were stacked on the dresser and the lemon curtains were blowing gently in the breeze from the open window.

Was he having another of his secret phone calls? There was an extension in the bedroom and I tiptoed upstairs, sure I was going to find him out at last. This time, I promised myself, I would tell Mum.

His bedroom door was ajar, the telephone still in its cradle, lying beside the bed. No J.B.

Puzzled, I pushed open the door of my bedroom and there he was, sitting on the bed. His shoulders were slumped and his face was drawn and grey. He looked older than I'd ever seen him. As if he'd had a shock.

Something had happened to Mum! That was my first thought. Until I saw what he was holding in his hands.

My diary.

He had been reading my diary.

He looked up at me slowly, not surprised or shocked to

be caught, but very deliberately. He'd been waiting for me. He looked at me as if he was disgusted by what he saw.

'What kind of girl have you turned into, Lissa?' He held up the diary. 'How could you have done such a terrible thing? How could you have been so cruel?'

I shrieked at him, refusing to feel guilty. 'You had no right to read my diary. That's private!' I tried to snatch it from him but he held it high away from me.

'Maybe so, but I'll tell you this, Lissa. You are going to school tomorrow and you're going to confess everything.'

CHAPTER TEN

All that night I screamed and screamed at him, but he wouldn't change his mind. 'You're going to own up to what you have done, and that's all there is to say.'

It was no use appealing to Mum. She'd never go against J.B. 'I don't know why I find it so hard to believe you could do such a thing,' she said, clutching a snivelling Margo against her. 'You did the same thing to little Jonny's poster. How could you have been so cruel?'

'You don't know how cruel Ralph Aird can be. He deserved it.' I refused to feel sorry for Ralph now, or guilty. He had brought it all on himself.

When I said that J.B. jumped to his feet. 'Deserved it!' he yelled at me. 'Deserved to have his hard work ruined, something he'd put so much of his time into ripped to shreds.' I could have answered him then, told him about what I'd put up with from Ralph, all the time he was in prison. Told him how he'd made a fool of him for working in Burgers A GoGo. But he didn't wait for an answer. Didn't want one. He took a step toward me. 'What could he have possibly done to deserve the wrath of you and your snobbish little friend?'

'Don't you say that about Diane.'

He didn't listen. 'Maybe you both suddenly realised he was better than you. And he was going to prove it by winning that competition.'

'He's not better than me,' I shouted. 'Ralph Aird's the scum of the earth.'

I sounded like Diane when I said that. Scum of the earth.

'And what does that make you?' he shouted back.

There was no arguing with him. No getting round him.

'I won't tell, and you can't make me.'

'Yes, I can.' He held up the diary. 'If you refuse to confess of your own accord, I'll hand this over.'

That was the worst threat of all. All my feelings, my hopes, everything was locked in the pages of that diary. I had no doubt he'd do what he threatened.

'You're the one that's despicable. Reading someone else's private diary. No wonder I hate you.'

That got to him. He sank on to the arm of the chair. 'Hate me then. I shouldn't have read it, I know that. But when I saw it lying there I thought maybe inside I'd find the key that might get me through to you. I just wanted us at least to begin to respect each other again, Lissa. I didn't know you hated me that much. I didn't expect to find anything like this.'

'I'll never respect you again. I hate you.' I was crying now. Didn't want to but couldn't help it. I didn't see any way out of the nightmare he was creating for me.

'Don't say that, Lissa.' Mum put her arm gently on my shoulder but I shrugged it off.

'I'll go with you to school tomorrow,' J.B. said quietly.

'To make sure I go?' I snapped.

'No. I want to support you.'

That almost made me laugh. 'You! An ex-con. Oh yes, I really need your support.'

'I'll go anyway,' he said.

'But Jonny . . . your interview,' Mum reminded him.

He looked up at her and managed a smile. He could always manage a smile at Mum. 'I'll go after. It'll be all right.'

But it wasn't all right. It was the most humiliating day of my life. To stand in the headmaster's office and have to admit to him, my voice shaking, exactly what I'd done.

Murdo was there too, and that made it a hundred times worse. His eyes were hard and cold as he stared at me. I tried not to look at him, but as a vampire in a ghost story his eyes pulled me towards them.

'But why would you do such a terrible thing?' he asked when I'd finished.

'He was always horrible to me.' It sounded stupid even as I said it. I wanted to get back at Ralph Aird, but that would have meant telling them about J.B.'s stupid job and Ralph's dad in the same prison as he was and I just couldn't say it. I wanted to cry, but I held the tears back and only said again, 'He's horrible.'

Murdo sighed. For once he didn't fly into a rage or throw things or pull at his hair. He only said in a soft Highland lilt, 'You weren't in this alone.'

I glanced at J.B. I had already expected this question. So had he. And I had told him again and again that I wouldn't bring Diane into it. That was the least I could do for her.

'But why not?' he had yelled at me. 'She's every bit as bad as you. She egged you on, I could tell that in the diary.'

But I wouldn't tell on her. It was the one thing I could do that was right.

I swallowed and lied. 'There was no one else involved.'

Murdo shook his head violently. 'No. No. She was in it with you. Tell me, Lissa.'

But I wouldn't budge. You don't grass on your friends.

I was suspended from school for a week. That was bad enough, but worse was to come. As I was walking through the empty playground on my own (I refused to leave with J.B. and he had hurried on for his interview), Diane came rushing up to me. Her lips were white with anger.

'Where have you been?' she demanded. But she knew. The news had travelled through the school like an inferno. 'If you've been telling on me, I'll say you lied. I'll never forgive you.'

I tried to tell her I hadn't but she wasn't in a listening mood.

'Anyway, I didn't do anything. You did it all yourself.'

'Diane I know, I wouldn't . . .' But she only pushed me away.

'If that's all you think of our friendship you can just forget it. I don't want to be friends with you any more.'

And though I called her back, she ran off, wouldn't listen.

That was the worst thing of all. Diane was no longer my friend. That was finally what made me cry in the quiet solitude of my room, away from everything. I cried because I had lost the only friend I had. I had lost Diane.

If I'd had the nerve to run away from home then, I would have.

I was suspended for a week.

No one phoned to ask where I was.

No one phoned to find out when I was coming back.

No one cared.

My only consolation was that J.B. didn't get the job. He pretended not to be disappointed when the letter arrived. But he was.

So was Mum, but she looked at me as if it was my fault.

'Your mind wasn't on the interview, Jonny.' I heard her comfort him. 'You had so many other things to think about.'

The main other thing being me.

Well, J.B., we all have problems, I felt like telling him. I had been expected to go to school, sit exams, do well, when the front pages were full of your trial and your guilt and your villainy.

You've just got to get on with it.

Anyway, I had lots to think about myself.

Like going back to school.

CHAPTER ELEVEN

My mum offered to come with me the morning I went back to school, but I said no. The last thing I needed was to walk in through the school gates protected by my mother.

So I went alone. Knowing I would be alone the whole day. I wouldn't even have Diane.

It was even worse than I could have imagined.

As I neared the gates I could see them all waiting for me. All the pupils in my year. They were standing on the pavement forming two lines across from each other. To get into the school I would have to pass between them. They were silent as I approached, so quiet it was terrifying and if I'd had the courage I would have run away then. But all I could do was to walk towards them, my whole body shaking.

Murdo had once told us about 'running the gauntlet'. I

never thought then that one day I would have to do it myself.

I stepped between the rows and held my breath. They didn't shout. They didn't scream at me. What were they going to do? Harry Ball was the first. He produced a whole bagful of rotten tomatoes and threw them at me. They splashed straight on to my face, into my hair. I let out a yelp as they exploded against my lips. I gagged and tried to spit them out but they were on my tongue, in my mouth, down my throat.

That's when I started to run. Then they all took their turn, pelting me with every rotting thing they had, rancid pears and squashy bananas and more tomatoes. I tried to duck and dive and avoid them, but it was impossible. I tasted mould and tried hard to keep my mouth shut, but with every direct hit I let out a yelp and my mouth was filled with rotten fruit. I immediately imagined maggots crawling down my face, wriggling round my tongue. I was crying out and I began to run faster through that angry crowd, dying to be past them. The smell was all over me, in my hair, in my clothes. I'd turn from one side and only get hit from the other. And all the time not a word, not a murmur escaped their lips.

At the end of the line, there was Nancy and Asra, their

faces grim. They pelted me harder than the rest. Nancy spoke the only words. 'I never thought you could be this bad.' And she let go with another handful of tomatoes straight into my face.

I ran, crying, heading for the toilets. Ralph Aird hadn't been in that crowd, and I was soon to understand why. He was standing at the revolving doors that led into the main school. I hesitated when I saw him, sure he was waiting to throw something even more disgusting at me. I would have to pass him, and I've never been so afraid in my life. He had a look of such venomous hatred. He spat in front of me. 'I'll show you, Blythe. You're goin' to be sorry.' It was all he said, but it made me even more afraid.

And then, suddenly from behind me, all of my year came sprinting forward. I was so sure they were after me again and I almost tripped through the doors and into the main school. They wouldn't dare touch me there.

But they weren't interested in me any more. They drew Ralph into their circle, Nancy and Asra and the rest and pulled him away, laughing.

And that's when I understood.

Ralph had not been one of the ones who had pelted me. They had made sure of that. If I told on them, and I suppose they expected that I would, no blame would be attached to Ralph Aird. Now, it was being made very clear to me that Ralph Aird was one of them. I wasn't.

I cleaned myself up as best I could in the toilets, all the time knowing I could get rid of the smell, but I would never rid myself of the humiliation. No matter how hard I scrubbed.

The door of the toilets squeaked open and I held my breath. Was this someone else to torment me? I dried my eyes quickly with a paper towel and swung round to face whoever it was.

It was Diane.

She stood at the door, one foot casually crossed over the other, her arms folded, just staring at me.

Diane hadn't been one of those at the school gates, but was she going to throw something at me now? I couldn't have borne that.

'You're in a mess,' she said. She kept staring at me. The suspense was awful. What was she going to do? Finally she let out a long sigh. 'You didn't tell on me, did you?'

'Of course I didn't,' I said at once.

And then she smiled. Or did the sun come out? At that moment they seemed like one and the same thing.

'I knew you wouldn't.' She came toward me and started brushing down my blazer. 'Well, that should prove to you the kind of people who are in this school. Not our kind of people at all.'

She linked her arms in mine. 'Come on. We'll show them. We don't need people like that.' She laughed loudly and wrinkled her nose in disgust. 'Scum of the earth.'

Everything was all right again. Diane was still my friend.

And did I need her! Because no one else was talking to me. As we walked along the corridor, anyone we passed turned away from me. They hardly looked, they never smiled. That was to be my punishment. Every one of the pupils in the school was a part of it. No one was to talk to me. I was to be ignored. 'Sent to Coventry' I believe is the stupid expression.

I didn't care. I had Diane. We walked to each of our classes, arms linked, while she whispered insults about them all and made me giggle.

Murdo's class was the one I was dreading most and as we filed in they all turned from me one by one.

Murdo was at his desk, and despite my efforts I was still in a mess.

'What on earth happened to you?'

I sensed they were all waiting for me to tell on them. They were expecting it. I hesitated, wanting them to worry for a bit.

'There's such a lot of rubbish in this school, it's very hard to avoid rubbing against it.'

Diane giggled, and so did I. The rubbish I was referring to was the rest of my class.

He didn't answer that. He knew what had happened. He most probably thought I had got everything I deserved.

What surprised me was that he didn't mention the collage or me, or Ralph Aird. He went through his lesson as he always did and when the bell rang he dismissed us. All of us except Diane and me. He motioned to us to stay behind and we stood at his desk while everyone else filed out.

'Why me?' Diane mouthed. I shrugged. After everyone had left he closed the door quietly and came back to where we stood at his desk.

'What you did to Ralph Aird was despicable, Lissa. But I know you weren't alone.' His angry eyes turned to Diane. 'And you're too much of a coward to even admit it. Well, I'm going to tell you thisss, Misssy!' Now his spit was directed on Diane. She sucked in her cheeks and I could see how angry she was too.

'You don't have the right to reprimand *me*. I haven't done any –'

Murdo's hands gripped the desk lid and I saw his knuckles grow white. 'Don't you dare interrupt me, girl!'

And with that he lifted the lid and smashed it down so hard even the glass in the windows shuddered. 'I want you both to know that I will be watching your every move from now on. Now get out of my sight before I get *really* angry.'

I didn't want to see him *really* angry. So I was off, pulling Diane behind me.

'I hate that man!' Diane said as soon as we were safely out in the playground. She was shaking with fury.

I was angry too. 'I hate him as well.' He would never let me forget what I'd done, and I hated him for that.

Diane pulled me round to face her and stared so hard at me that I blinked. 'No, Lissa. You don't understand. I really hate that man.'

And she said it with such venom I was afraid.

CHAPTER TWELVE

May 10th

Here I am writing in my diary again when I swore I never would. But I have to. I don't know why but writing things down seems to make them clearer to me. And so much is happening. Only now, I'll keep my diary well hidden. I won't ever risk J.B. finding it again.

He's been acting very suspiciously, since the business with me which he caused, no one could deny that, and not getting that job, which I also got the blame for by the way. He also lost his job in Burgers A GoGo. He didn't fit in, the manager had told him. I could have told him that ages ago. He's ancient compared to the other waiters. He's just been moping around the house since then. I heard Mum trying to talk to him the other morning before she went off to work. Her voice was filled with worry. Snatches of, 'You can't go on like this.' And, 'Something else will turn up.' And most significantly, 'You can't go on blaming yourself.'

And then, yesterday, something changed. There was a phone call, just after I came in from school. His voice was soft as he answered it and that made me suspicious right away. Then he told me to keep an eye on Margo, he had to go out for a while. He was back within half an hour, but there was something different about him. I couldn't figure out what it was until today when he was striding about the house, doing the housework, hoovering, yet all the while concentrating hard, as if his mind was on something else entirely.

He had a purpose.

Has he got the chance of another job? If that's the case, why hasn't he told Mum about it?

Or is it something else? Something dark and sinister and called Magnus Pierce?

It was. I know that now. But at that time, I had enough to worry me just going to school every day.

'Could someone partner Lissa here?' Miss Day, our science teacher, looked around the classroom. Everyone else was working in pairs but as usual I was on my own. When Diane wasn't at school I was always on my own. And Diane wasn't at school today. She was off for her interview at Adler Academy and the thought that I might soon be losing her scared me. I just had to get into Adler Academy too.

'I said!' Miss Day tapped the desk with her pencil. 'Can we have a partner for Lissa Blythe?'

Everyone found somewhere else to look. Since that day when I'd come back to school not one of my classmates had broken breath to me. Most of the time I didn't care. I had Diane. Even though our friendship was frowned upon by Murdo, who disliked both of us now, and by J.B. He wanted me to stop seeing her altogether. He might have been able to stop me seeing Diane after school – and he had. But he had no power over who I was friendly with in school. Especially since, thanks to him, I had no other friends.

But on days like these it would have been pleasant to have someone to sit with in the canteen during lunch, instead of eating by myself at a long empty table. Listening to the throb of conversation and not being able to join in.

'No one wants to be my partner, Miss,' I told her.

'Nonsense, Lissa!' and just then to my utter astonishment and terror, Ralph Aird stepped forward.

'I'll be her partner, Miss.'

Miss Day beamed. 'Ah good, Ralph. That's what I like to see, turning the other cheek.'

Miss Day lived in a born-again Christian world, but I was afraid that if I turned the other cheek to Ralph Aird he'd most probably punch it.

Ralph Aird came to my table without a word. There was a smug look on his face – but there was always a smug look about him now. As if he'd won something over me. Now, he had friends galore. He was included in every group, smiled on by teachers, especially Murdo who was always involved in deep conversations with him. Now, he never missed school. I had begun to think I had done him a favour destroying that collage.

Yet I still remembered the way he had spat out those words at me. 'You're goin' to be sorry.' And he still made me afraid.

Ralph Aird had been a wasp up my nose for too long to think he'd just fly off without stinging me. Every night I waited to hear our old car's windows being smashed, or maybe I'd wake in the midnight dark and sniff, sure I could detect the smell of petrol being poured across the doorstep before he set our whole house ablaze.

All I knew was he was planning to do something.

I held my breath as he came toward me. Would it be today? An accident in the science lesson? I glanced at a jug of maggots Miss Day had ready for one of her experiments. I had a sudden nightmare vision of Ralph Aird grabbing them and pouring them down my throat. There would certainly be plenty of people willing to hold me down while he did.

'Can't have wee Lissa on her own, can we?' he said sarcastically.

'Doesn't bother me,' I told him.

''Course it does. You used to be the big shot. And now, look at you. Not a soul's even talking to you.'

He was trying to goad me but I wouldn't listen.

'Don't care.'

Still he couldn't let it go. 'Nobody likes you, Lissa. But do you know what I tell them? Because I'm always sticking up for you.' He sniggered. 'I tell them,' his voice was soft, so soft Miss Day would never hear him, 'I tell them to feel sorry for you. Because you're pathetic. Really pathetic.'

And that's when he really got through to me. Not with his hate, and not with his threats, but I just couldn't, wouldn't take his pity.

I looked around for something handy, and there it was, that big jug of maggots. I lifted it and before he knew what was happening I had tipped the whole squirming lot over Ralph's head.

You could have heard him yell in California. He did a war dance and shook his head wildly. The maggots were everywhere. The whole class went wild. I was screamed at and called every horrible name under the sun. It was lucky I was in Miss born-again Christian Day's class or I would probably have been expelled. As it was, I was sent to the headmaster and reprimanded. I didn't care. I'd shown Ralph Aird that there was nothing pathetic about me!

But I just had to get out of that school. I screamed that at Mum when she got home that night. 'Why can't I go to Adler Academy?' I yelled.

'With Diane Connell?' J.B. said softly. He was already shaking his head. 'The sooner she goes there the better. Get you two separated and maybe both of you will behave like human beings.'

'She's the only friend I've got!' Why couldn't they understand that? They both knew that no one spoke to me at school any more, except Diane.

'That's your fault,' he had the nerve to say. 'It's up to you to prove you're not as bad as they think.'

That was rich coming from him. 'Like you, I suppose.'

He stood right in front of me, making it impossible for me not to look at him. 'I want to tell you something, Lissa. I brought you up to think you were better than other people. I worked hard, but I wanted money and more money. So you could dress better than other people, live in a better house. Have better holidays. Material

98

things, Lissa. I thought that's what was important. I brought you up to think that too. But it's people who matter, Lissa. I've tried all my life to get away from my background, from the poverty I had when I was a boy. But I'm going to tell you something you don't know.' He hesitated, and sat on the edge of the sofa so that his eyes were level with mine. 'You never knew your granny, my mother. She died before you were born. But do you know what she was, Lissa? She was a cleaner in the schools. She worked really hard all her life. You should be proud of her. I should have been proud of her. Instead, I was ashamed. I wanted something better – and I didn't care how I got it.'

Why did he have to tell me these things now? He'd never told me this before. Why now?

'You still want to go to Adler Academy?'

Mum stepped in angrily. 'It's out of the question anyway! Adler Academy costs money!'

'That's OK. He can pay for it with his new job.'

I'd caught him off guard. His face flushed red, his eyes darted to Mum's.

'What new job?' she asked.

'Didn't tell you about that, did he? Didn't tell you about the phone calls either, eh? Or the sneaky visits somewhere.

Must be a new job . . . a new job with an old boss, called Magnus Pierce!'

And I ran out of the room and upstairs and the last thing I heard before I slammed my door shut was Mum's worried voice. 'Jonny, not again. What's going on?'

CHAPTER THIRTEEN

May 29th

I met Magnus Pierce today as I walked home from school. I'm sure he was waiting for me. His big Mercedes was parked by the kerb. I knew it was his by the registration plate. MAG 1. I would have crossed the street to avoid him but by the time I noticed his car I was too close. And anyway, suddenly he stepped from the car and held the door open so that it blocked my way. He was so tall, so broad, so threatening. Yet, anyone seeing him with me would have thought he was, perhaps, a favourite uncle.

'Lissa!' he said, as if in total surprise. The street was alive with people, brushing past me, rushing to catch buses, but suddenly, I felt very alone. 'I'm so glad I met you. You can pass a message on to your dad. Tell him to give me a call, will you? Let me know how he's getting on.'

Doesn't he realise I know they've been phoning each other? I didn't say that, of course. I didn't say anything.

He asked how things were with me, but I only shrugged my shoulders. And then he said something that shocked me.

'They'd be better if you were going to that Adler Academy though, wouldn't they?'

Does he know everything? Of course, he must. J.B. probably tells him.

Though, when I got home, he pretended to be surprised when I told him. No, more than surprised, horrified. Good actor, J.B.

'You met Magnus Pierce!' he said and he grabbed me by the shoulders, looking all concerned. As I said, good actor.

'Yes. And he insisted I tell you.'

And he had. As he stepped back into the Mercedes he had said softly, 'You take care going home now. These days you can't be too careful.' Then he smiled his bright white scary smile. 'You make sure you tell your dad I was speaking to you.'

'Don't ever talk to him again,' J.B. snapped at me.

Who is he trying to fool? Does he think I haven't noticed his suspicious behaviour?

'Please, Lissa, Magnus Pierce is dangerous. I'm doing my best to protect you. If only you knew . . .' He sounded so sincere I almost believed him, except that as soon as I was in the kitchen pouring myself some milk there he was back on the phone, his voice a whisper.

I had passed the message on. 'Get in touch, J.B.,' Magnus Pierce had said. And he had.

After that day, everything seems to have moved so fast. Like a rocket spiralling out of control. I remember the next day so well.

I had never seen Murdo so smug. He strode up and down the class, saying nothing. Humming some tuneless Highland lilt. You always know when Murdo is angry. He bellows, he throws chalk around the room, he slams down his desk, spittle bursts through his clenched teeth. And his hair goes wild.

And you always know when he's happy. Because he hums tunelessly, just as he did that day. As we all trooped into his classroom he beamed at every one of us, even Diane and I. It was all very fishy. The whole class knew that something was in the wind but he waited until we were all seated before he decided to put us out of our misery.

He rubbed his hands together, gleefully. 'I have wonderful news. Wonderful news,' he said in mounting excitement. And when Murdo got excited he could spit for Britain. 'Our school has received a great honour. We should be very proud. The Council has chosen one of our number to design its new Millennium Logo. One of our number. Someone in this class. I wonder if any of you can guess who it is?'

But we didn't have to guess for long, because Murdo's smile focused on only one person. Ralph Aird.

'Come here, Ralph, and stand beside me.' He opened his arms to welcome him and Ralph stood up sheepishly. He had a look on his face that was a cross between smugness and embarrassment.

'Come here, Ralph,' Murdo said, 'and bask in some glory.'

Ralph shuffled towards him.

Murdo continued. 'Our Ralph has been commissioned. Commissioned, mind you.' He pointed a stubby finger at Harry Ball. 'Tell me what commissioned means, boy!'

Harry spluttered trying to think of an answer. 'Is it something to do with a prison sentence, sir?'

The class fell about laughing. Even Ralph Aird giggled.

Murdo raised his eyes hopelessly. 'You may be a whizz kid at maths, Harry, but your command of the English language is deplorable. Commissioned!' he explained to us, with some extra spit, 'in this case means he's getting paid for his work!' There was a gasp from the class.

Ralph stood up straighter, pride written all over him. Murdo slapped him on the back. 'Yes. We have a professional artist in our midst!'

Murdo began to clap then and, without hesitation, so did the rest of the class. Not hesitantly, but with enthusiasm and pride, like I'd never heard before.

'Good on ye, Ralphie boy!' someone shouted.

'Terrific!' Nancy called to him.

Even Asra stood up and gave him an extra special cheer.

Of course it was all Murdo's doing, I told myself. Working behind the scenes, making sure Ralph's potential wasn't lost forever. But as I listened to the class applauding, and watched their faces, their genuine pleasure for Ralph's success, I felt alone. None of them had spoken to me in weeks because of what I'd done and I hated them and yet, here they were delighted for Ralph Aird of all people.

I looked at him beaming like an idiot and I realised with dismay, I was jealous, jealous of Ralph Aird. In that same moment, he looked at me. He always looked at me with disgust, as if he hated me and for a second that was the look he gave me. And then, the look changed to a puzzled frown and then gave way to a smile that spread across his face. And I knew he could read the envy in my face.

Diane leaned toward me and tugged on my arm. 'He probably only got it because they felt sorry for him. He's a loser.'

'WHAT WAS THAT!'

Murdo's voice boomed out and the applause died in an instant. Silence fell. Total silence.

Murdo took a deep breath and strode up the aisle to where Diane sat. 'Stand up, Miss Connell.'

Diane flushed and licked her lips.

He stopped right in front of her.

At first I thought she was going to refuse but after a moment she got to her feet, defiance in her every move.

'Now, why don't you share with the class what you just said?'

Diane wouldn't even meet his gaze. She didn't answer him, but I could tell by the nerve throbbing in her cheek just how angry she was.

'Forgotten already, have you?' Murdo looked round at the rest of the class who had all turned to face him. 'Shall I tell you what she said?'

He turned back to Diane. 'Diane Connell says that Ralph only got that commission because the Council felt sorry for him. Did you hear that, Ralph?'

Even then his gaze never left Diane.

I glanced at Ralph and his smile had disappeared.

Murdo continued. 'This is our Council, by the way, which evicts old ladies from their homes if they can't pay their rent. This is our Council, which throws blind people out of our libraries when they try to bring in their guide dogs.' He batted his eyes in feigned shock and the class began to snigger. 'Ooo, but they're all heart when it comes to our Ralph. Och, they decided, the poor wee laddie. Let's give him this commission. He's rubbish but we just feel so sorry for him.'

Now he was laughing too. He smiled over at Ralph. 'Och, isn't that nice, Ralph?'

For a moment he let the class laugh. Laugh with him, and laugh at Diane. And Diane didn't like it one bit.

Suddenly his voice became an angry roar again. 'Do you know what your problem is, Diane Connell? The only way you can feel important is to belittle other people. And I am telling you now, and I genuinely hope it helps you to know this, that true greatness comes from recognising other people's worth. Maybe then, you can find your own.'

He stared straight at her. I knew, because I know the kind of teacher Murdo is, that he really did want her to understand that. He wanted to change something in Diane. But Diane wouldn't look back at him. She kept her eyes downcast, and sucked in her cheeks as if she had something sour in her mouth.

Finally, he shook his head. 'Stay behind after class, Diane. I want to talk to you.' And he began to walk back down the aisle to Ralph.

And suddenly, the class were applauding again, only this time they were applauding Murdo.

I stood at the door while Murdo spoke to Diane. His voice was soft at first, but grew steadily louder when he realised he was getting no response from her.

'Lass! I'm only trying to help you!' he yelled at her. 'Do you want to go through your whole life being totally obnoxious?'

Diane tutted in that superior fashion of hers and looked away with a long sigh.

'I will not have you speaking to me like this,' she said.

Murdo's eyes went wide and he roared so loud I thought he was about to invade England. 'I will speak to you any way I choose, lassie, if it's for your own good. And you can bring your father here and I'll tell him the same thing. Do you hear me!!!!' With that Murdo lifted the desk lid as high as he could and banged it down ferociously. Diane jumped and so did I.

'Ach, get out of my sight, lassie!' Murdo bellowed at her. 'And if your behaviour doesn't improve I'll be sending for your parents.' And Diane swung round and left him.

'Thank goodness I'm going to Adler Academy!' I'd never seen her so angry. Tears were starting in her eyes but she kept swallowing them back. 'Trying to humiliate me in front of the whole class. Who does he think he is? Well, he's just stepped over the line. I'll get my own back on him.' She suddenly pulled me back to face her. 'And you're going to help me.'

'Me?' The thought did more than dismay me. It terrified me.

'Yes, of course, you. I helped you get back at Ralph Aird. Now it's your turn to help me get back at Murdo.'

She turned from me then and I shivered. It was a warm May afternoon, but it was Diane who made me shiver. There was something really scary about her.

'I'm going to make him very sorry he ever treated me like that.'

CHAPTER FOURTEEN

May 31st

I can't think what Diane is planning for Murdo. What can you possibly do to a teacher? No one's ever going to believe anything a pupil says, especially a pupil like Diane. Though I didn't say that to her. I hope she just forgets about it. Murdo's anger never lasts. He used to hate Ralph Aird too. I can remember him bellowing at him when Ralph had done something particularly nasty – which was often. Once, he even ran him all the way to the headmaster's office when he caught him trying to flush Harry Ball's gym shorts down the toilet. Trouble was Harry Ball was wearing them at the time.

And now look at Ralph. You would think he was Murdo's favourite. And all because one day he'd caught him doodling a sketch of him in his English jotter.

We'd all held our collective breath expecting Murdo to yank Ralph to his feet and frogmarch him out of the school.

Instead, he held it up for all the class to see and he said, 'Ralph Aird, that is extremely good.'

After that, whenever Ralph had an essay to write, Murdo insisted he illustrate it as well. So Robinson Crusoe came to life on the pages of Ralph's exercise book and Shylock the money-lender, and Dr Jekyll and Mr Hyde. And Ralph came to life too – until the day I destroyed his collage.

I told all this to Diane, hoping it would make her see that Murdo had no real favourites and that once he spotted her potential she'd be his darling!

But nothing I said could calm her down. 'He had no right to say he'd inform my parents if my behaviour doesn't improve. Who does he think he is? He's nothing but a big Highland savage. How dare he speak to me like that.'

What she said frightened me. But the way she said it frightened me more. Because she sounded just like me. Arrogant, sure she was better than everybody else, looking down her nose at the rest of the world.

Belittling people to make her feel important. Murdo's words came back to me.

I was glad to get away from Diane for once. Diane frightened me today.

Was that only yesterday I wrote that? So much has

happened since, it seems like an age away. I went downstairs after I'd finished writing my diary and I found Mum crying in the kitchen. Mum never cries, and that scared me.

'What's wrong? Has something happened?' I asked her.

But she wouldn't say.

'It's him, isn't it?' I jerked my head towards J.B. in the living room. 'What's he done?'

'He's done nothing, Lissa,' she snapped at me.

There was an atmosphere all through our meal. Mum hardly spoke and she even scolded Margo when she tried to stuff her dinner into the back of Jonny's fire engine. She usually laughs when Margo does that. I've heard her giggling as she lifted one of Jonny's trucks and an avalanche of mashed potatoes and mince cascaded from the back. Last night, Margo was scolded and the poor little thing looked puzzled and hurt.

J.B. put his hand over Mum's and squeezed it. And do you know what? She pulled her hand away. I've never seen her do that before. Something was going on, but what?

It was midnight when I woke up, thirsty. I was still half-sleeping as I stumbled out of my room and made my way downstairs for a glass of milk.

As I passed the living room I heard his whispered, furtive voice. J.B. was on the phone.

I crept closer and listened.

'I hope you know the risk I'm taking,' I heard him say softly. Then after a pause when the other person was obviously speaking he added, 'You'll protect me? Now, where have I heard that before?' He didn't speak then for a moment and I realised by the odd 'OK', 'Yes' that he was listening to instructions. It was his final words that told me everything I needed to know.

'I told you. I'll do what you want. I know when I'm beat.'

Forget the glass of milk. I took the stairs two at a time to get back into my bedroom before he came into the hall.

But I couldn't sleep. I couldn't. Because it was all happening again. He was going back to work for Magnus Pierce. He'd tried to keep away from him, but now, without a job, he knew he was beat. Soon, he'd be back in prison and Mum couldn't take that for a second time.

Why was he such a fool? Would he never learn? No wonder Mum was crying. I never hated him so much as I hated him last night, knowing he was going to ruin what little we had.

And I couldn't do a thing to stop him.

There was an atmosphere in the house this morning too, and I only added to it. I couldn't look at him. I only heard

Mum say one thing to him, and it just confirmed what I already knew. 'I don't want you to do this, Jonny. It's too dangerous.'

And his whispered answer. 'I don't have any choice, Liz.'

The phone rang while I was forcing down some breakfast and I held my breath as Mum answered it.

'Lissa, it's for you. It's Diane.'

With a sigh of relief I hurried to the phone. Diane's voice was a torrent of breathless whispers. 'You promise you'll back me up this morning. No matter what?'

'Diane, what's wrong?'

But she didn't answer me. 'I can't talk now. But just you promise. Anything I say . . . anything!' She repeated it through gritted teeth. 'You agree with me. Promise?'

'What is it you're going to do?' I felt sick to my stomach. She was planning something. Something terrible, I just knew it.

'Can't talk any more. Have to go.'

And the line went dead.

I was angry with the world this morning. That's my excuse. No one cared about me. Not my parents. Certainly not J.B. None of my classmates. They didn't even talk to me any more. And definitely not Murdo. It seemed I, along with Diane, was the only one of his students who lacked potential.

Diane was the only friend I had. I couldn't risk losing her. No matter what she'd planned I decided, I'd be behind her one hundred per cent.

Mr Becket, the deputy head, was waiting for me at the school gates. He stood with his arms folded, his face stern. 'Lissa Blythe!' His voice was as grim as his face. 'The headmaster's office. Right now!'

'What's up now?' I demanded. I wasn't in the mood to be polite. It had to be something to do with Diane, but at that point I was more angry than nervous.

I was kept in the headmaster's outer office while Mr Becket stepped inside to announce my arrival. The secretary pursed her lips at me in an angry frown.

What had Diane come up with? I began to sweat and could feel guilt written all over my face. Mr Becket appeared at the office door. 'Inside,' he ordered.

With as much confidence as I could muster, I marched into the office.

But my confidence took a real knock when I saw what was waiting for me.

The headmaster was standing behind his desk and his face was grim. Beside him, Murdo. He was ashen-faced as if he'd just had a terrible shock. And there in front of them, sitting in two chairs, were Mr Connell and Diane. She was crying, sobbing back tears. When she heard me come in she jumped to her feet and rushed toward me. She held out her hands and I saw, for the first time, that they were bandaged.

'Oh, Lissa. I'm so glad you're here.' She grabbed at the lapels of my blazer. 'Tell them,' she was pleading with me. 'Tell them you saw everything. You heard everything.' Her shoulders heaved with her sobbing. 'Tell them it was him.' Now she pointed one of her bandaged hands at Murdo. 'He did this! Tell them he slammed down the desk on my hands . . . and you saw him doing it!'

CHAPTER FIFTEEN

Mr Knowles, the headmaster, beckoned me forward. Now, I was sure it was me who was ashen-faced. 'I think we'll hear this from Lissa herself,' he said sternly.

Diane clutched at my arm. 'She saw it all. She'll tell you exactly what happened.'

Mr Knowles snapped at her. 'Keep quiet, Diane.'

But she didn't. She babbled on nervously, telling me everything I needed to know to back up her story.

'He was so angry with me. I've never seen him so angry. And he made me put my hands in the desk and then . . . he slammed it down on my fingers. He'd made me stay behind after class. And he's never liked me, ask anyone. He doesn't like Lissa either.' She turned to her dad then. 'We don't belong in this school, Dad. Neither of us.'

Mr Knowles looked at me. 'We must know the truth, Lissa. This is a very serious allegation.'

My mouth was dry. So dry my lips were stuck together. I couldn't have answered in that moment if you paid me. I looked at Diane, crying, squeezing my hand. Like my friend? Or was that a warning to back her up?

I looked at her dad. He was holding his anger in check. He believed his daughter without question. Would J.B. have as much faith in me? Somehow I didn't think so.

And then my eyes fixed on Murdo. If only, at that moment, his look had been soft, repentant. Pleading even. Reminding me of how much I liked him, deep down.

But Murdo's eyes were full of that fire he was so famous for. He didn't look like a sheepish little Highland terrier, so much as a Rottweiler ready to go for my throat. He didn't expect, or want my sympathy. He only expected the truth. Nothing else. But, there was something else in that look. It only took a second for me to know what that 'something else' was. Murdo wanted the truth. And he wasn't expecting to get it. Not from me. Not from Lissa Blythe, who was always lying. Who had destroyed Ralph's precious collage. Whose father was a crook.

Fine, I thought. I won't let him down.

My voice trembled when I answered. 'It's all true. I saw everything. I saw him do it just like Diane said.'

Murdo drew in a shocked breath and his eyes never left me. I could feel them burning into me, although now I couldn't hold his gaze. Instead, I looked at Mr Connell. He was nodding, as if he had only been expecting me to confirm Diane's story.

Suddenly Murdo exploded, doing his own case no credit at all. 'Tell the truth, Lissa! You know that is a downright lie!'

But his sudden outburst had only proved, to Mr Connell at least, that all we said was true.

'This is the kind of man you allow to teach children!' he demanded of Mr Knowles. 'Well, let me tell you, I will make sure he will never teach children again. I'll go to the authorities. I'll go to the papers. I have connections, Mr Murdoch. I intend to sue you. I intend to sue this school. You picked on the wrong student when you picked on my daughter.'

Diane glanced at me, she wasn't crying now. She'd won and her look seemed to say; 'told you he'd be sorry.'

I felt as if I was caught up in a horrible nightmare. This wasn't happening. This couldn't be happening.

Mr Knowles turned to Murdo. 'I'm sorry, Mr Murdoch.' His voice was soft. 'I'll have to suspend you while this matter is being investigated.'

Diane began crying again. 'Why do they have to investigate it, Daddy?' She crumpled into her father's arms, still holding on to me. 'Why won't they believe Lissa? He's always bringing her down, Dad. Belittling her.' She used Murdo's own word to condemn him. 'Belittling me too. They're going to try to make us out to be liars, Dad. Just because Lissa's dad's been in jail are they going to hold that against her for the rest of her life?'

I felt whatever colour was left drain from my face. Diane was clever, cleverer than I'd ever imagined her to be.

Mr Connell pulled me to him protectively. 'Indeed they will not. I won't stand for it.'

'We will give everyone a fair hearing, Mr Connell,' Mr Knowles said deliberately. 'No one in this school will be branded a liar unless it can be proved beyond doubt. But Hamish . . .' he corrected himself. 'Mr Murdoch is one of our most popular teachers. His reputation is at stake. His future as a teacher. Of course this has to be investigated.'

Mr Connell was furious. 'He has no future as a teacher. I'll make sure of it. The mud from this will stick. A man like that, with a temper like that, should never be in charge of children. I'll make sure he never teaches again.'

Murdo didn't flinch. Instead he stood taller.

I was the one who shrank inside.

Murdo not a teacher? He's the best teacher I've ever had. He brings a lesson to life with his passion and his anger. And teaching is everything to him. We had once asked him what he would do if he wasn't a teacher and I will always remember his answer.

'Ach, you can put me in my coffin and bury me deep if I can't teach.'

And because of me, he might never teach again.

And still I couldn't open my mouth. I couldn't bring myself to tell the truth.

Now, I began to cry.

Diane hugged me close. 'Look what he's done, Daddy. Now he's made Lissa cry.'

'You take Lissa out of here,' her father ordered. 'I have things to discuss with these . . .' he hesitated, 'these teachers.'

She hugged me all the way from the office and once we were safely out of earshot she whispered in triumph, 'Told you I'd get him, didn't I?'

I lifted her bandaged hands and looked at them. 'Did you do this to yourself?'

She grinned. 'It was worth it. Old Murdo will never teach again, not now.'

CHAPTER SIXTEEN

June 1st
What have I done? What have I done?

Did I really only write that this morning, only a couple of hours ago? I've spent that time, sitting here on my bed re-reading my diary and going through all the events that have led up to today. I see now how I changed when Diane came into my life. Or was I always such a horrible little snob? Looking down my nose at people, hurting them at every turn.

But no, I can't have been. Murdo said he'd never known me to be deliberately hurtful till Diane came along.

But I won't blame her.

Murdo always says take responsibility for your own actions. So from now on I will.

Murdo. He has taught me so much. Will he ever teach any student anything again?

He said that Diane belittled people to make herself seem important. That true greatness comes from recognising other people's worth.

He always did recognise other people's worth. From Harry Ball with his mathematical brain, to Ralph Aird.

He made even the dumbest person in his class feel they had something to offer.

There was never a teacher like Murdo.

And I've just ruined his life.

My diary told me something else too. How J.B. changed after he read it. Read how I hated him, read how horrible I'd become, read of the terrible thing I had done to Ralph. And when he read how much I wanted to go to Adler Academy he knew he'd need money to send me there. The kind of money he could only earn by working again for Magnus Pierce.

The mysterious phone calls had begun in earnest after that. He had seemed to come to a decision. To have a purpose. The purpose being to turn back to crime.

And I had driven him to it.

Magnus Pierce and Diane. They had a lot in common. Both of them wanted to rule people's lives. They both made people do bad things.

J.B. and I have a lot in common too. I see that now. He

didn't tell on Magnus Pierce out of some false sense of loyalty. And I backed Diane up for the same reason.

Take responsibility, Murdo says.

Now is the time for me to do that.

I can change things, or I can at least try.

I can't let J.B. work for Magnus Pierce again. It would kill my mum. She's been happy since he's been home. How can I convince him he doesn't have to? But if he's already told Magnus Pierce he would work for him, he can't go back on that. Not with Magnus Pierce. So, no good talking to J.B. He won't listen. He can't. He's caught up again and can't get out. Like a fly caught in a web.

But maybe if *I* ask Magnus Pierce. Beg him to let J.B. go, let us get on with our lives. Maybe I can do something. I have to try.

If I want to change things I have to go straight to the spider.

Magnus Pierce.

Luckily, Dad was at the nursery with Margo so as I left the house there were no awkward questions, no need for more lies. I paused for a moment at the front door.

Dad. I had called him Dad, and it hadn't been painful at all. My dad.

I took the bus to the far side of town where Magnus Pierce's offices are.

'You know where to find me,' he had said once. And I did too. J.B. used to work there, in a brightly lit office, with phones and faxes and computers constantly linked to the Internet. All very businesslike and above board. Fronting a business that relied on fraud and smuggling and all sorts of dodgy dealings.

Magnus Pierce's Mercedes, MAG 1, sat in the driveway heralding his presence. Good. I wanted him to be there. I wanted to ask, beg him if I had to, to let J.B. go. We didn't need the money. And surely he didn't need J.B.

It was only as I climbed the winding staircase from the street entrance that I began to grow really nervous. I had rehearsed over and over in my mind what I was going to say, but now as I took one faltering step after another my mouth went dry and my mind was a complete blank. All I knew was that it was up to me to get J.B. out of this mess.

A long corridor at the top of the stairs led to Magnus Pierce's office and I could hear murmured voices behind the closed door. One of them was his. Louder than the other. In charge as always.

Even before I knocked on the door it was hauled open by a tall woman, very thin, her black hair streaked with grey. It took her only a moment to recognise exactly who I was.

'Hey, it's the Blythe girl,' she called back into the office, then she stood aside to let me pass.

He was sitting behind his desk, and he swivelled round in his chair to look at me. He had his jacket off and his tie was loosened. Papers were strewn on his desk, and he looked for all the world like a proper businessman and not . . . not what he was.

No wonder at first he had fooled J.B.

'Lissa.' He beamed a smile at me with what looked like genuine warmth. 'And to what do I owe the pleasure of this visit?' He gestured me to a seat and I took it nervously.

The woman closed the door behind her and leaned against it. She looked unfriendly and her hooded black eyes never left me. She was scary.

'C . . . could I speak to you alone?' I tried to sound confident, but my voice was too shaky. 'Please?' I added.

Magnus Pierce nodded in the direction of the scary woman. 'Give us a minute, Esther.'

She looked none too pleased to comply. 'She's Blythe's daughter,' she said. 'I might want to hear this too.'

Magnus Pierce's eyes flashed a warning at her. It warned

me too. She wasn't a visiting girlfriend, or even a customer. She was one of them. And she didn't like J.B.

I watched her as she pulled the door closed.

Be calm, Lissa, I told myself. Speak clearly, don't get excited.

Yet, as soon as I opened my mouth my words came out in a torrent.

'It's about my dad.' There. I'd called him it again. Not too hard. 'I know he's coming back to work for you.' He raised an eyebrow and I hurried on not wanting him to think Dad had told me anything. 'It's OK, I know he's not supposed to talk, and he hasn't. I heard him on the phone to you. Late at night, when he thought we were all sleeping. He didn't tell me. He didn't tell anyone. So you know you can trust him. He went to prison for you, didn't he? He didn't say a word then. I thought he was stupid doing that, but he thought he was doing the right thing. I understand that now. But you can't let him come back to work for you. I don't care if we never have any money. But I couldn't bear him going back to jail.' Still Magnus Pierce said nothing. He rested his chin on his folded hands and just looked at me.

'I know he's going to do what you want. I heard him tell you that last night. But please, let him be. You don't need him to work for you.'

Now, I got some kind of reaction, even if it was only that he sat straight in his chair. 'And when is he going to do all this for me?'

'I don't know. Soon. That's why I had to come.'

Esther suddenly threw open the door. 'I told you never to trust Blythe.' She'd been listening to my every word. 'Have you been talking to Blythe?'

Magnus Pierce's voice was icy. 'I told you. He wouldn't talk to me. Wasn't interested in any of my offers.'

'And if you haven't been talking to him, who has?'

I was baffled. Magnus Pierce hadn't been talking to my dad? So who were all the phone calls coming from? Who had he been meeting?

Magnus Pierce gave me the answer. 'Who else?' he said. 'The police, of course. They've been after him since he came out of jail. Trying to get him to tell what he knows. And he knows plenty.'

They were talking as if I wasn't there.

'Now it seems he's ready to share what he knows with them,' Esther almost yelled. 'You've got to do something to stop this, Magnus.'

I was trying to take all this in. Dad hadn't been planning to go back to work for Magnus Pierce after all. He'd been planning to do what I'd always wanted him to. Tell the police everything he knew. Mum wouldn't want him to do that. She'd know how dangerous it would be. No wonder she'd been crying. It all fell into place. The furtive phone calls weren't from Magnus Pierce at all. They were from the police. They would protect him, they had said; but then, who could protect him against the likes of Magnus Pierce? I began to breathe faster when I realised I had just ruined everything. I had walked into the spider's web and told him all he needed to know. If I'd done nothing, things would have been all right. How could I have been so stupid?

I stood up. 'Maybe I'll just go,' I said hopefully.

Esther pressed her hand firmly on my shoulder and pushed me back into my seat. 'I don't think so.'

Magnus Pierce smiled and lifted the phone. 'Send a car for Jonathan Blythe. Bring him here. And don't take no for an answer. Tell him his daughter Lissa has just paid me a visit.' He turned his chilling gaze on me. 'And I'd never forgive myself if anything happened to her.'

CHAPTER SEVENTEEN

I'd done the wrong thing again. I thought I was saving Dad from Magnus Pierce's clutches and all I'd done was pull him into more trouble.

As we sat silently waiting for him to arrive I tried to plan my escape.

I could scream, but who would hear me? These offices were far from the main road, surrounded by building sites. I could make a run for it. Somehow I didn't think I'd get very far. Esther was leaning against the door, barring my way.

The best form of defence is attack. Could I throw myself at Magnus Pierce, take him by surprise? Another stupid idea. I could just picture that giant of a man holding me at arm's length, or lifting me by the collar while she stood watching in amusement.

This close, I saw how big and powerful and scary Magnus Pierce really was.

What had made me think I could appeal to his better nature? This man didn't have any better nature. And now, Dad was caught like a rat in a trap, because of my stupidity.

Magnus Pierce swung himself round in his swivel chair to face me. 'Won't be long now, princess.'

'I'm not your princess,' I snapped at him.

He smiled broadly. 'Spirit,' he said to Esther. 'That's what this one's got.'

She wasn't impressed by my spirit. She scowled at me. 'I told you we should have dealt with Jonathan Blythe a long time ago.'

'He went to prison because of you!' I shouted at both of them. 'He never told on anyone. So why can't you just let him be!'

Magnus Pierce shook his head. 'Ah, your father has always been hampered by a conscience, Lissa. Bad thing to have in our business. Sooner or later, he would have passed on his information.' He held up his hands. 'Now, we can't allow that.'

'Don't bother explaining anything to her. She's only a child.'

And the way Esther was looking at me I didn't think she intended for me to get any older.

The clock on the wall ticked the seconds away with the beating of my heart.

What were they planning to do to us? When Dad came would they just let us go? Somehow I didn't think so.

Were we going to 'disappear'? I'd heard of people doing that. Without a trace, never heard of again.

And if we did, Murdo's life would be ruined forever because I'd never get the chance to tell the truth. Tell them that Diane's story was all a lie. That Murdo was the best teacher in the world.

I promised if I survived today, that's the first thing I would do. Save Murdo.

It all seemed a hundred years ago and yet it had only been this morning.

I looked at the clock. Only ten minutes had passed. Had the car arrived for Dad yet? Was he being forced to leave the house? I could have almost cried as I imagined him trying to organise a babysitter for Margo. He'd never leave her alone under any circumstances. Never had since he'd come out of prison. While Mum worked he had cooked and cleaned and looked after us and I had never appreciated anything. The job at Burgers A GoGo must have been as humiliating for him as it had been for me, but he had been willing to suffer it just to have a job. And what had I done? Made things even worse for him. Just as I was doing now.

And what was he doing now? Was he struggling with the men Magnus Pierce had sent to collect him? Was he being dragged out to a waiting limousine? Maybe the neighbours would see. His struggles would alert them. They might call the police.

But of course, they wouldn't. They knew Dad's past. Who he had been involved with. They would probably think he was just being arrested again by some plain-clothes police.

There was no way out. The car arriving at the house would have taken him by surprise. Magnus Pierce had given him no chance to contact the police himself to tell them what was happening.

It took me all my time and effort not to cry.

And suddenly, after an age, he was here! I could hear him pounding up the stairs before bursting into the office, his eyes wide with alarm.

'Lissa!' He dragged me close to him. 'Did they hurt you!'

'Of course not.' Magnus Pierce sounded offended. 'What kind of people do you think we are?'

'I know exactly what kind of people you are.' Dad held me even closer. 'Magnus, let Lissa go. Please. That's all I ask.'

I struggled. 'No. I'm not going to leave you. It was me who got you into all this.'

From behind us Esther was laughing. 'Let you go? Are you joking?'

And Magnus Pierce just shook his head sadly. 'I'm afraid, Jonathan, that is out of the question now.'

I began to shake, I couldn't help it. Dad pulled me closer against him.

'What are you going to do with us?' he asked.

We never did find out.

Because at that instant all hell broke loose in the office. The whole place was suddenly swarming with policemen and women, bursting through doors, pounding up stairs.

Esther gasped and tried to rush past them but she was grabbed and held.

Magnus Pierce's face was ashen. He took a step back and looked from Dad to me, puzzled. It was all over in panic-stricken seconds. Handcuffs were snapped on Magnus Pierce's wrists. He didn't struggle. He looked straight at the detective who held him and said coldly, 'I'll be out of this in days. You know that.'

The policeman grinned at him, and glanced at Dad. 'Will he, Mr Blythe?'

Dad's voice was sure with his answer. 'Not this time,

Magnus. You were holding my daughter against her will.' His voice was unforgiving. His glance moved to the policeman. 'I'll tell you everything you need to know.'

Magnus Pierce's eyes narrowed viciously and didn't leave Dad until he was pulled out of the office.

When he had gone, Dad let out a long, exhausted breath. 'How did you know we were here?' he asked the policeman.

'We've had a man watching this office for weeks,' he told Dad. 'When he saw this young lady,' he managed a smile in my direction, 'running inside, looking, shall we say, slightly upset, he contacted us and even before we got here he saw you being escorted into the building by a couple of Pierce's heavies. He said you looked even more upset than your daughter. It wasn't too hard to put two and two together.'

Dad held me close, and for the first time, I let him. He was shivering. 'I was so frightened he'd hurt you. I couldn't think why you'd gone to see him.'

'I thought you were going back to work for him,' I mumbled. 'When you read my diary you changed. As if you thought all I wanted was money, to go to Adler Academy, to get my old life back.'

He squeezed my arm. 'It was reading your diary that did change things, Lissa. I realised the same thing that had happened to me was happening to you. You were being drawn into doing things by someone you thought was a friend. Keeping your mouth shut. Protecting Diane Connell the way I had protected Magnus Pierce. You made me see how wrong that was. That's when I decided to tell the police everything I knew. No matter how dangerous it might be.'

When he spoke again, his voice was choked with tears. 'You've been caught up in a horrible world, Lissa, and it's all my fault. No wonder you can't forgive me.'

But I had created a horrible world of my own, and I couldn't blame anyone else for that.

I hugged him closer. 'Don't worry, Dad. It's all over now.'

He shook his head. 'With Magnus Pierce it will never be over.'

CHAPTER EIGHTEEN

But he was wrong.

Oh yes, Magnus Pierce got out on bail, and we were all afraid.

But he was the one who 'disappeared'. It was suspected at first that he'd fled the country, but that turned out to be wrong too. Because a few days later a body was found, wrapped in a tarpaulin and buried in a shallow grave. Magnus Pierce had made many enemies and he could never be relied upon to keep his mouth shut the way my dad had.

Yes, my dad. Easy to say it now. He cried the night we heard, not for Magnus Pierce, but because of the dark and sinister world he'd drawn us into. A world, he said, we should have known nothing about so young.

'It's all my fault,' he said, over and over. 'How could I have been so stupid?'

But I understand now, how you can get caught up with

people, led astray, believing you're not doing anything that's *so* bad.

Diane Connell was my Magnus Pierce. And the day after all that excitement I had to go into school and tell the whole truth. I had to stand there, in front of Murdo and Mr Knowles and admit I had lied. Knowing that my lie could have ruined his life. I expected Murdo to bawl at me, rant and rave at me in his anger. But he surprised me again. He only shook his head and pursed his lips and when he finally did speak it wasn't what I expected at all.

'It took a lot of courage for you to come here and say this, Lissa. Thank you.'

And that was when I cried. I bubbled like a baby. Murdo didn't come near me to comfort me and the headmaster only looked embarrassed.

'Yes. Yes. Go on, have a good greet,' Murdo said. 'Let it all out.'

Diane never came back to school. She's not going to Adler Academy either. After what happened it seemed they rescinded – is that the right word? They withdrew their offer anyway.

I did try to phone her. To explain to her what I'd done and my reasons. But it was her mother who answered.

'Diane isn't here,' she told me in clipped angry tones. 'And we don't want you phoning here again.'

I was suspended for a week though I know Murdo didn't even want that. I didn't mind. Too many things were happening at home anyway.

It was the longest week of my life. I had no idea how the rest of my class would take what I had done to their favourite teacher. I was dreading going back that day.

June 12th

Murdo was waiting for me at the school gates when I arrived this morning. I deliberately came late, terrified of having to run yet another gauntlet. I waited round the corner till I heard the bell and only made my way to school when my class had safely filed inside.

And there was Murdo.

His hair has grown since I last saw him and it stood erect around his head like a burning bush. 'Ah Lissa, good,' he said as if he was surprised to see me. As if I didn't know he had been waiting. 'You can help me carry some books into class.'

After what I had put him through he was protecting me. Making sure I walked into his class with him by my side. I thought it was such a thoughtful thing to do I almost cried again.

'You've come through a lot over the past few weeks, Lissa,' he said as we carried copies of To Kill A Mockingbird to the classroom. 'You've learned a lot too.'

He knows about Magnus Pierce, of course. It's been in all the papers, although our involvement in his arrest has been suppressed by the police.

'Yes,' I said. 'With what I've learned I could write a book.'

Suddenly, he bellowed a laugh that echoed through the high long corridors. 'That's it! You'll be a writer.' Then he added with a mischievious twinkle, 'You certainly know how to tell a tall tale.' And he sprayed me all over with those 'T's.

A book, I thought. My 'potential' at last? Well, I've practically written one already with this diary, haven't I?

So I actually had a smile on my face as I walked behind him into the classroom. The ordeal to come almost forgotten for a moment.

Almost, but not entirely.

I stayed as close to Murdo as I dared and put my pile of books down on his desk.

It took every ounce of courage I had to turn round and face that class. Each of them was looking straight at me and I could read nothing in their stony faces except hate.

They were never going to talk to me again. Or, did they have a worse punishment in mind? I bit my lip and began walking toward my desk.

What happened next absolutely stunned me. In a million years I couldn't have guessed it.

One by one, the class began to clap, slowly at first, until every one of them was applauding me. Just the way they had applauded Ralph that other day so long ago.

Even Ralph Aird was clapping. Maybe not so enthusiastically as the rest, but he was clapping just the same.

I looked around them in amazement, so sure they were winding me up but no. The smiles on their faces were genuine, so were their shouts of praise.

'Good for you, Lissa,' Nancy told me with a smile.

'You did the right thing.'

Asra patted me on the back as I passed her. 'Couldn't have been easy. Good for you.'

I looked round at Murdo, and he seemed as surprised as I was. This wasn't what he had expected either. But the smile on his face showed it pleased him too. And suddenly, he was applauding along with everyone else.

This will go down in history as the best day of my life.

They all spoke to me at break, Nancy and Asra, welcoming me back to their little circle. We're all going swimming at the weekend, and I really think if I try hard enough, we can all be real friends again. Real friends, not like Diane.

It was while we were talking that Ralph Aird slouched

toward me, hands in his pockets. I held my breath.

'I'm sorry about what I did to your collage,' I told him right away. 'I'm really sorry.'

'So you should be,' he said in that surly voice of his. He hasn't a clue how to accept an apology.

I told him too that I'd been waiting for him to do something awful back to me.

He leaned against the wall and stared at me. He was chewing gum and blowing bubbles. Trying to look cool, as usual. 'I planned to,' he said. 'Don't you worry. I kept thinking about all the rotten things I could do to get back at you. But nothing I came up with was bad enough.'

I swallowed. Wondering if he had something bad enough lined up by now.

He spat his chewing gum on the ground in front of me before he spoke again. 'But see that day Murdo told the class about me getting commissioned, I watched your face, Lissa Blythe. And do you know what? You were jealous of me. And see, right at that minute,' he poked his finger at me for emphasis, 'I knew old Murdo was right. Success is the best revenge. And I decided right then I was going to design the best logo anybody's ever seen and make you green wi' envy.'

He laughed right into my face. 'And see next year, I'm going in for that competition again and I'm going to make an even better collage, starting today – you see this time . . . I'm going to guard it wi' my life.'

I didn't tell him then, but I had already decided to help him. I stayed behind after school and together we pinned up the long banner that stretches right round the classroom walls. A blue banner. Blue for peace.

I even helped him pin on the first character.

'Not blinking Harry Potter again,' I wailed when he brought it in.

He only sneered. I don't think we'll ever get on, Ralph Aird and I, but I'll tell you something strange. Something I only realised today.

Diane Connell was wrong about a lot, but she was right about one thing.

Ralph Aird is dishy.